THE WORST SHIP IN THE FLEET

Book One of Dumb Luck and Dead Heroes

Skyler Ramirez

Persephone Entertainment Inc.

Cover design by: Warren Design

Kindle ISBN: 978-1-964457-00-0
Print ISBN: 978-1-964457-14-7

Printed in the United States of America

Publisher: Persephone Entertainment Inc.
Texas, USA

To anyone who has ever lost faith in themselves. It could be worse. You could be Brad Mendoza.

Also to the Bacas and the Knights, for encouraging me weekly to write and for being my excellent alpha readers.

CONTENTS

FOREWORD

I'm having so much fun writing this series.

On the surface, *The Worst Ship in the Fleet* is an action-adventure with a touch of comedy, a story of space battles, crimes on naval warships, mystery, and desperate measures in the face of impossible odds. It's a tale of a damaged man whose internal monologue and behavior make us simultaneously laugh and cringe. Brad Mendoza is irreverent, brash, apathetic, self-deprecating, and pretty much always drunk.

Jessica Lin, on the other hand, is intelligent, beautiful, self-assured (at least sometimes), and determined to do the right thing. But she harbors her own deeply damaging secrets.

Their personalities are so different that they appear to be the proverbial oil and water. But (and I'm sure you can see where this is going) they end up having to rely on each other totally, and they quickly find that neither has much hope for a future without the other.

As with all my books, this story has no graphic scenes or swearing. But that doesn't stop us from delving into some fairly serious adult topics, presented in a way that I hope doesn't offend. Because above everything else, *The Worst Ship in the Fleet* is a story of redemption: two people who seem so irretrievably damaged find that there is no depth so low that a comeback isn't possible.

In essence, there is a little bit of Brad and Jessica in all of us. We've done things or had things done to us that we regret and wish we could erase. We've faced inflection points, large and small, where we must choose to either let our pasts dominate us or fight on and forge a new future. It is my sincere desire that, along with some entertainment, some laughs, and maybe some eye rolls, you will find a message of hope in these pages.

So, sit back, kick up your feet, and enjoy *The Worst Ship in the Fleet*.

Thanks,

Skyler Ramirez

CHAPTER 1

Dead-End Assignment

"**B**rad, you're an idiot."

I looked at the lined face of Admiral Terrence Oliphant. His crisp blue uniform held so many ribbons that I was idly wondering how he kept from hunching forward under their weight all the time. I wanted to argue with his statement; I really did. But you didn't argue with Terrence 'Terrible' Oliphant in the Promethean Navy unless you had a death wish.

But that alone didn't stop me from vocally disagreeing with the man. I had to admit I actually did sort of have a death wish, and not strictly in a figurative sense. The last six months had been the worst of my life in more ways than I could count... in no small part because of the man sitting across from me. But even so, I chose not to argue with his assessment of my intelligence, mostly because he was right.

I *was* an idiot. If the last six months had taught me anything, it was that my stupidity was an incontrovertible fact. Oh, sure, after this meeting, I would grumble about how Old Man Oliphant had screwed me over, but I honestly knew I deserved every bit of his criticism. That was the problem.

"You know, I should just kick you out of the Navy." He let the statement hang there as if he expected me to finally rise to my defense or beg for my job. As with his earlier insult, I didn't engage with him on this either. Part of me was absolutely terrified that he might follow through with his threat. But the other part of me wanted it to happen. It would remove the one final excuse I had to try to be...well, anything.

In my mind's eye, I pictured myself leaving the Promethean Naval headquarters building in street clothes, my rank and station stripped, and my fate sealed. I knew what I would do if that happened, and it involved a large bottle of cheap whiskey and my service sidearm. Maybe I would leave a note; maybe I wouldn't. Who would read it?

Obviously seeing I wasn't going to give him the satisfaction of begging to stay in the Navy, the Admiral frowned deeply. Then he shrugged and continued. "I would kick you out if it were entirely up to me. But it's not." He seemed incredibly disappointed in that fact. "Besides, I think you'll find yourself wishing I *did* drum you out. Maybe you'll even save me the paperwork and resign your commission." Now he sounded hopeful. But despite my fatalistic musings, I wasn't about to resign—no way would I give him that satisfaction.

"Your new assignment is being sent to your implant now. We're sending you to Gerson."

Hmmm. Maybe I needed to reconsider that whole resignation thing. Gerson was the hole of the spacelanes, the armpit of Promethean territory. And it was on the edge of human-controlled space. It literally bordered on *nothing*. So, *nothing* ever happened there. It barely even rated a naval station. Still, maybe it was better than eating a bullet...just barely.

"You'll be taking command of the *Persephone*," he continued, a smile breaking out on his too-good-looking features for the first time.

And there it was. Now it definitely wasn't better than just ridding the universe of my pathetic existence. The *Persephone* wasn't a command; it was the butt of a joke. It was the last of the Poseidon-class missile frigates, a failed experiment in building smaller warships to extend the Promethean Navy's patrol area, an experiment that had lasted just long enough for the first Poseidon classes to show their stripes in their shakedown cruises. They were horrible. Not only had their experimental ion drives proven so unreliable that they were never put in another Navy vessel afterward, but their meager armament and small missile magazines made them next to worthless in a fight with anything larger than a garbage scow. And even then, it was preferable if the garbage scow was already damaged and running on autopilot to give the Poseidons more of a fighting chance.

Persephone had been old when I graduated from the Academy. And her reputation back then had already been secured. No matter what assignment my classmates and I had received for our first post-graduate cruises, the common refrain had been: 'Well, it could be worse. At least it's not the *Persephone*.'

Worse, *Persephone* was such a small ship, with so small a crew—even at capacity, the Poseidons only held two dozen spacers—that she barely rated a lieutenant commander in the command chair. And I was a full captain.

The message was clear. The Navy wanted Brad Mendoza out. But they weren't going to just discharge me and let me fade to obscurity in peace. They wanted to *embarrass* me on the way out.

Still, I said nothing, and Oliphant's Cheshire Cat smile eventually faded as I refused to take the bait. It was a small victory.

"Get out," he finally said. "I expect you off planet and en route to Gerson within the hour. Dismissed."

I stood, threw a sloppy salute—going through the motions but too numb to be either respectful or overly disrespectful—and turned to leave.

"Oh, and Brad…" his voice stopped me in my tracks. I turned back around to see a hard look on the old man's face. "Stop calling Carla. She wants nothing from you ever again. Understood?"

Words failed me, so I just nodded and turned again to leave. It really sucked to have one of the most senior admirals in the Navy hate your guts. It was worse when he was your father-in-law…well, *ex*-father-in-law.

CHAPTER 2

My New Boss Hates Me

"Sir, we'll be docking at Gerson Station in twenty minutes."

I opened one eye to regard the young spacer third class who had nudged me awake. I hadn't actually been sleeping, but pretending to doze was an excellent way to avoid interaction with the crew and few other passengers on the small transport that had carried me the three days through jump space to the outer limits of human territory.

They were judging me—all of them. I had caught a few of the enlisted spacers whispering and casting glances at me early in the journey. And sure, they could have been talking about my unshaven appearance or my wrinkled uniform. But I couldn't shake the feeling that they *knew* about my latest assignment and were having a great joke at my expense.

Because as much as it would be a drag to serve aboard a naval transport like this one, each and every one of the spacers and officers on this bucket could still say the same thing: 'At least it's not the *Persephone.*'

Or translated another way: 'At least I'm not Brad Mendoza.' But *I* was, and it wasn't fun at all.

I mumbled something back at the spacer who had roused me, and he went off to wake up the transport's other two remaining passengers on the final leg to Gerson. One of them was an older enlisted man wearing an engineer journeyman's patch, telling anyone who saw him that he might be enlisted, but his unique skillset made him pretty much immune to the orders of any mere mortal officer below the rank of commander. Shiny new ensigns who made the mistake of trying to issue an order to an engineer journeyman usually learned quickly the very narrow extent of their true authority over such men and women.

He had ignored me the entire flight in such a pointed way that I was one hundred percent certain he knew exactly who I was and where I was headed. It simply wasn't natural for him to have never once looked my way in three days.

The other passenger was a civilian, or at least she wasn't in uniform. But she was very pretty, with long auburn hair and a lithe build that showed curves in just the right places and reminded me a bit of my ex-wife. She had caught me looking *her* way a couple of times on the first day in transit, letting my imagination run a little free. Her sour return look quickly put an end to my fledgling fantasies. Since then, I had made it a point not to look at her; every time I did, even by accident, she met my gaze with a hard stare that told me she wouldn't want my attention even if I weren't the biggest pariah in the Promethean Navy right now.

I sat, studiously trying not to see or be seen by either the engineer or the redhead while the transport neared Gerson Station. At least, as the ranking officer on board the ship, I was granted one of the few seats near a virtual portal. It was the one and only concession to luxury that the spartan naval transport provided—the bathroom didn't even have a shower, just a full-body disinfectant and deodorant sprayer that made me crave the bottle of cheap scotch I'd smuggled in my footlocker—but the portal gave me a video view of the approaching station.

Unfortunately, it also gave me my first look at my new command.

HMS Persephone probably hadn't started life as the spacecraft visual equivalent of a flounder, but she sure had evolved into it over the decades. Where once her paint scheme might have been a uniform gunmetal gray or even the matte black of a Navy warship, now she was a patchwork of discolored hull plates that were evidently being held in place by chewing gum and maybe a few toothpicks. She looked like a kindergartner's wild drawing of what a warship might look like...if that kindergartner was terrible at art and hated the Navy and everyone in it and wanted them to collectively die from embarrassment.

My new home in space was shaped roughly like a long box, with an unevenly tapered front end and a flare at the back for the ion drive nozzles. On her dorsal hull, she had a small conning tower with an observation pod at the top of it. As with most warships, that observation pod had the only windows on the ship. It was designed as a last-ditch place for the ship's officers to visually target enemy craft if their entire AI targeting system failed or their external sensors were all fried. Of course, that was ridiculous; anything that could take out both the AI and the ship's external sensors would surely take out the thick glass enclosure of the observation pod well beforehand.

It was the same basic structure of most human warships—function over form. But somehow, *Persephone* made it look so much uglier than any ship I'd ever seen. And it wasn't just the patchy paint scheme. There was something depressing about her lines, as if the hull plates themselves weren't aligned properly to each other, making her look like an old beat-up car one of my buddies had in high school that I swear started life as parts of four different vehicles.

I was frankly surprised they even let *Persephone* keep the *HMS* prefix. I very much doubted His Royal Majesty wanted the ship in front of me to be associated with his name, his Navy, or even the same galaxy he lived in.

When the transport docked at the station, I wordlessly grabbed my day bag and returned a hasty salute from the spacer at the airlock before disembarking. I had very few privileges left to my rank, but having the transport crew unload my footlocker and bring it to *Persephone* for me was at least one thing I could still count on as a captain in His Majesty's Promethean Navy.

No one from the station had come to greet the transport as it docked, so I stepped out into an empty corridor. The cute but mean redhead and the aloof engineer journeyman would disembark after me—another supposed privilege of my rank. It didn't matter that even the lowliest spacer third class had a better chance of being in the Navy six months from now than I did. The military was nothing if not securely tied to tradition and ceremony.

I absently rubbed at the stubble on my chin as I hefted my day bag over my shoulder and walked down the short corridor to wherever it led. Most stations were designed the same, so the door at the far end would probably empty me out into a customs and immigration entry point, but maybe Gerson Station would surprise me with something different.

It didn't. The bored-looking man at the customs and immigration desk eyed me with just enough interest for me to know that he knew who I was and why I was there—the lack of respect in his tone also made that clear—before he waved me through.

"Oh, Captain Mendoza," he said, almost as an afterthought. "Captain Wainwright has asked that you present yourself at the Naval Commander's Office on level three before you board your ship."

I eyed the man dubiously. I had no idea who Captain Wainwright was. His or her name was probably in the orders and briefing packet stored in my implant, but I hadn't even been tempted to read them beyond the first few sentences. Those had made it clear I was to report to *Persephone* in the Gerson system and end my naval career, with the admiralty's compliments, of course.

Shrugging, I walked out the far door and into a larger open area than I'd yet seen. It looked like the interior of any other station, with a few shops and moderately narrow corridors between them, interspersed with intersections that led to other docking airlocks. Except, being a Fringe system, the shops in Gerson station were low-end and utilitarian. There were no luxury goods being sold on this station, at least that I could see. Apparently, people this far out from the rest of humanity didn't need fancy luggage, purses, or perfumes. They were good with packaged fried foods and cheap booze. My kind of place.

The signs stenciled on the corridor bulkheads led me to the station's central hub, where three cylindrical lifts clustered together to take people to different levels. I boarded the one facing me and keyed in level three using an old-style button after my implant failed to find a connection to the lift's controller. How quaint.

Two minutes later, I was off the lift and stepping through the door into the outer room of the Naval Commander's Office. This part of the station *did* look like every other station I'd been on, all standard naval issue. The carpet here was a little more worn than usual, and the reception desk had a few extra chips in the cheap plastic veneer, but otherwise, it could have been a station in orbit of Prometheus itself.

I eyed the spacer behind the counter, a young man who watched me back with barely concealed interest. He was trying very hard not to gape at me and frown at my sloven appearance, and he was failing miserably at both.

"Can I help you, Captain?"

I fought the urge to sigh. The kid had to know precisely why I was there. His passive-aggressive question just showed that I was to be afforded no respect befitting my rank. Six months ago, that would have ended with me pulling the boy up and dressing him down while conducting a point-by-point inspection of his uniform while I questioned his parentage. Now...I couldn't even muster up enough righteous indignation to care.

"Captain Mendoza to see Captain Wainwright," I said in what I thought was a long-suffering tone. But it sounded monotone to my ears. I'd had a hard time expressing any emotion in my voice lately. Everything just came out flat.

"Of course, sir. I will inform the captain of your arrival. If you would please take a seat, I will show you in as soon as she is ready."

Now I did sigh. I just couldn't help it. Wainwright, whomever *she* was—at least I knew her gender now—had summoned *me*. Which would imply that she'd known I was coming and had planned this encounter. Making me wait now was either a clumsy power move or a calculated insult. Either way, it didn't bode well for the meeting I was about to have.

I dropped my day bag onto one of the empty chairs and flopped myself down in the one next to it. Pulling up a game on my implant, I moved a bunch of stupid shapes around to try and get them to fit in a stupid box. It was mindless, but it was about the most complex thing I could get my brain to tackle these days. And at least it kept me from thinking about anything for a few minutes here and there. Thinking was generally dangerous for me.

After ten minutes or so, right about the time I had

restarted the game for the sixth time trying to beat my daily high score, the spacer at the desk stood and cleared his throat. "This way, uh, Captain."

I stood, leaving my bag where it was, and followed the young man to one of the doors behind his desk. He opened it and gestured for me to enter, which I did reluctantly.

Captain Wainwright was a sour-faced blond with her hair pulled back into a severe ponytail that made her forehead look huge. She had eyes the color and luster of puke, and her gaunt features made me worry that the Navy's ration shipments to Gerson must be a few months behind schedule. She frowned as I entered and threw her a salute that was only slightly less sloppy than the one I'd given my former father-in-law the last time I'd seen him—when he'd ended my naval career in all but name.

"Captain," I said expectantly. Well, I tried to sound expectant, but I think I just sounded bored...or maybe medicated, even though I hadn't been able to get a drink on the station yet.

"Captain," she replied, her frown coming through twice as intensely in her voice. I pretended to ignore it, which was easy because I really didn't care.

Without waiting for an invitation, I moved further into the small office and plopped down in one of the two spindly chairs that faced her across the desk. I was gratified to see her frown even more deeply at my impropriety. I'd had so little joy lately, but seeing her upset gave me just a hint.

"What can I do for you, Captain?" I asked.

She waited a tick, though her eye twitched noticeably at my continued lack of decorum. I almost smiled. When she spoke again, her voice was heavy with her disapproval.

"I would welcome you to Gerson, but maybe we can dispense with the pleasantries and get straight to business."

I shrugged and said nothing, my thoughts turning again to the bottle of scotch in my footlocker. I'd passed at least two liquor stores in the station on my way here; maybe I could pick up another bottle or two. There was no telling how long I'd be onboard my new ship before there would be another opportunity to stock up.

"I'm sure you're aware of just how irregular this all is," Wainwright said as I daydreamed of an alcohol-induced stupor.

"Irregular?" I asked, seizing on the word.

"Yes, quite," she responded, then studied me again. She was starting to remind me of Admiral Oliphant, which didn't necessarily endear her to me. Even when things had been good between me and Carla, Terrible Terrence and I had never exactly gotten along. He had tolerated me so long as his daughter was in love with me, but the second she'd come to her senses, he'd dropped all pretense of liking or respecting me. At least Wainwright was skipping straight to the disdain and dislike. No pretense here.

When I didn't say anything else, she sighed and continued. "Normally, command in the system would go to the senior most captain, as you well know. But my orders are different in this particular case." She paused, eyeing me expectantly.

I thought about her words for a long moment, unsure of what she was getting at. Then a strange and rare moment of clarity hit me. I mentally commanded my implant to bring up Wainwright's service record and specifically asked for her date of latest promotion. Sure enough, she had been promoted to captain three years before, almost a full year after my own promotion date. So that made *me* the senior captain in the room. Awkward.

"Am I going to have a problem with you, Captain Mendoza?" she asked when I still said nothing. I think she was trying to sound stern, but her voice cracked a little at the end of the question, and in another startling moment of clarity, I realized that at least a portion of her cold demeanor toward me had to be from her own nerves. After all, it wasn't every day you met the most hated man in the Promethean Navy and realized that he *should* have been your commanding officer.

"Probably," I replied, shrugging again. "Everyone else seems to have a problem with me."

Her eyes widened in surprise. Whether that was

from my frank admission or my rakish good looks as I threw her a lopsided smile, I decided not to wonder.

She frowned again, which based on the lines etched on her face, must have been her default expression even when she wasn't sitting across from the Butcher of Bellerophon. But lucky for her, she had me in the flesh now, and I was giving her a real reason to frown. It must have been a fulfilling experience for Wainwright.

"I won't lie, Captain, you're nothing like I expected based on your service record," she said through her latest frown. "At least, your record before... the incident." She said the last word like she was suddenly sucking on a lemon, which might have been a better look for her.

I decided to say nothing again. Let her draw her own conclusions; they would be far better than the truth in almost any event. Me opening my mouth was unlikely to make much of a difference.

"Anyway," she said after a long moment, "I will be your commanding officer while you're here in Gerson. As I'm sure your orders have already made clear to you." They probably would have if I'd read them. For now, I'd have to take her word for it.

"I will expect weekly reports from you during patrols and daily reports while on station. Is that understood?"

I raised an eyebrow and almost smiled. I could tell she was expecting me to argue. After all, I was more senior, and the stated expectation of regular reports should have insulted me. Oh sure, it was standard procedure for me to give reports on a similar schedule to any commanding officer, but there was a fiction to maintain that I would do it out of my own courtesy rather than as the result of a direct order from an officer of my same—lesser really—rank. I decided to let it slide. I was just having such a hard time caring.

"Of course," I replied evenly. "Now, if I may be excused to report to my new command?"

She frowned again—her upside-down smile was growing on me by now—and nodded. "Dismissed."

I gave a jaunty little salute and left without saying another word. But as I grabbed my day bag and left the small office area, I felt my already low mood sink even further. Oliphant and the admiralty had not only sent me to Gerson, the veritable butt crack of human space, to command the worst ship to have ever flown His Majesty's colors, but they had added insult to injury by suborning me to a more junior captain.

Not that I could blame them. It really might be better for all involved if I just quit. I'd even started drafting my letter of resignation during the journey from Prometheus to Gerson on the transport. The only thing that had kept me from sending it was the image of the smile it would put on Oliphant's face.

CHAPTER 3

*What Have I Gotten
Myself Into?*

"Captain on deck!" the young ensign hollered as I stepped through the inner airlock door of Persephone. I winced. In the short walk from Wainwright's office to my new ship—which may or may not have involved a stop at a liquor store and a quick shot, or three, at a station bar—I had developed a headache. The ensign's shrill voice was like an ice pick in my temple. I already disliked the kid.

"As you were," I said, trying hard to make my voice not sound annoyed. I failed.

"Captain Mendoza," the boy said, lowering his rigid salute. "Commander Lin sends her regards and apologizes for not being here to meet you. We had expected you an hour ago, and she had to head down to engineering to confer with the Cheng about an issue with the ion drives."

'Cheng' was the near-ubiquitous shortening of 'chief engineer' that had been used on naval ships since time immemorial. It had probably originated on Old Earth even, but no one knew for sure. Besides, I'd only met even a handful of folks in my life who had ever seen Earth, much less knew anything about its naval history and traditions.

"Understood, Ensign..." I squinted down at his nametag, but he beat me to it.

"Stevens, sir. Ensign Peter Stevens. From Kipling. This is my first assignment, sir. And happy to be here."

No, he wasn't. Unless he was dumber than I was. But he was an ensign, so maybe he *was* stupid. Only time would tell. I just grunted at his fake enthusiasm.

"Very well, Ensign Stevens. I assume you can show me to my quarters?"

"Of course, sir. If the Captain would follow me?"

And follow him I did. It took all of four minutes to traverse half the ship to get from the airlock to the captain's cabin. And when we arrived there, I was underwhelmed. I'd seen larger officer cabins on modern patrol boats. The idiots who had designed the Poseidon class obviously hadn't even considered the comfort of their commanders. I'd been in showers bigger than the outer office of my new quarters. And I'm pretty sure I'd seen dog beds larger than the bunk in my new bedroom.

Shaking my head, I dismissed the overeager ensign with a wave of my hand and tossed my day bag onto the bunk. At least my footlocker was already in place on the shelf below my closet, though no one had bothered to remove and hang up my uniforms. I should have cared about that, I suppose, but made no move to unpack my things.

Looking around, I almost reopened that letter of resignation on my implant. But I had the fleeting mental image of the admiralty gleefully stranding me in the Gerson system by refusing me return transport to Prometheus on a naval ship, and I decided against giving up my commission quite yet. After all, I hadn't even had time to come to loathe my new ship yet, though it was certainly off to a strong start.

I looked at my day bag and was tempted to take out one of the bottles I'd purchased on the station. Stevens had no doubt smelled the alcohol on my breath from my stop at the bar, but he'd been wise enough not to say anything. Still, I was already feeling a bit buzzed, and even a screwup like me knew better than to show up to my station on my first day of a new command *completely* drunk. I'd wait until that evening.

A knock at my cabin door interrupted my heavy contemplation of the proper procedures of command.

"Come," I mumbled, but the hatch opened before

the person could have heard me. I stepped—and it indeed was just about one big step's distance—out of my bedroom and back into the outer office to see a large brute wearing an enlisted man's garb, with the chevrons of a petty officer on his skinsuit sleeves, which were rolled up against regulation to reveal beefy, hairy forearms. The guy had to be at least two meters tall, abnormal for a spacer. I imagined he hit his head all the time on the tops of hatches throughout the ship. He was also handsome, in a way that made me feel oddly threatened, with a square chiseled jaw covered in just enough stubble to enhance his appearance—I would have killed to look that good without shaving; I just tended to look...well, like an alcoholic. He had blond hair perfectly combed and slightly longer than regulation, above cold blue eyes. He reminded me of my high school bully.

"Captain Mendoza?" he asked in a voice that would have sounded belligerent if I hadn't known any better.

I looked around the cabin incredulously. Who did he *think* was wearing the captain's uniform in the captain's cabin?

He didn't wait for my response. "I'm Jacobs. I'm sure you've read my file." I had not. But that didn't make him special. I hadn't read *any* of the personnel files attached to my orders.

"So, you know who I am and what I'm all about,"

he continued, unaware that I most decidedly did not. "And I just wanted to talk to you early to...set expectations."

I frowned. "Spacer, you're bordering on insubordination," I said in my best attempt at a stern voice. It took a lot these days to make me feel any emotion, but this guy had instantly rubbed me the wrong way.

He smiled! "I don't care, Captain," he said flippantly, and my mouth dropped open. I'd always thought that was just a turn of phrase, but my mouth *literally* dropped open in surprise. Go figure. "Listen," he continued, "everyone knows who you are and what you did. They don't send captains they like to the *Phony*. So, I'll give it to you straight. You stay out of my way, and I'll stay out of yours.

"But don't think you can intimidate me with your rank, Mendoza. No one is going to listen to a performance writeup from the Butcher of Bellerophon." He was the first person ever to use that nickname to my face. I knew what they called me behind my back, of course, but the audacity!

"Stay out of my way Captain. And we'll get along just fine."

My mouth was still open, and I was debating how to respond when the big man turned heel and left back through the outer hatch, which he almost slammed closed behind him.

Stunned, I sat down hard in my tiny desk chair,

staring at the hatch and picturing the man's receding back. Never in my fifteen years of naval service had I even *heard* of an enlisted man talking that way to a *captain*. Oh sure, stories abounded of senior chiefs and petty officers dressing down shiny new ensigns and even the occasional lieutenant who got too big for his britches. But a *captain*? Never!

I wanted to be furious. I wanted to call the man back, read him the riot act, and then throw him in Gerson Station's brig for insubordination. But I was still so shocked by the encounter that I just sat there, staring at the closed hatch and wondering just what in the depths of Hades I'd gotten myself into.

CHAPTER 4

Jessica Lin

Five minutes later, I was still sitting mouth agape at my desk when another knock came at the cabin door. I jumped in my seat, involuntarily picturing the massive Jacobs having returned to spout more insults and maybe even break me in pieces with his hairy forearms.

But I overcame my shock when the knock came again; it sounded *timid* of all things. Definitely not Jacobs.

"Come," I said, and the hatch opened slowly.

In stepped one of the most gorgeous women I'd ever seen. Have you ever seen one of those women whose dimensions are so perfect that it hurts? And whose face is so wonderfully proportioned, with smooth unblemished skin that never needs an ounce of makeup, that it makes you forget your wife—well, ex-wife for me?

Me neither. But the woman before me came as close as anyone I'd ever seen on both counts. I'd always loved Carla and thought she was as beautiful as any woman in the galaxy. And maybe it had something to do with her telling me she hoped I'd die in our last conversation with each other, but the King's officer I laid eyes on now put Carla to shame! Her short hair was jet black and straight, a sign of her obvious Asian ancestry, along with the slight hint of epicanthic folds around her eyes. She wasn't overly tall—probably around 175 centimeters—but her thin waist and legs made her look taller than she was, while her curves offset them in an incredibly pleasing way.

"Captain Mendoza," she said crisply, throwing an equally sharp salute as she brought that perfect figure to full attention in a way that made me want to bless the King's Navy for designing its uniforms to double as decompression skinsuits. "Lieutenant Commander Jessica Lin, reporting for duty. Welcome aboard, Captain."

I stared at her, my mouth open—twice in one day!—before I finally mumbled, "At ease, Commander."

She dropped her salute and put her arms behind her back, shifting her stance wider on the deck and keeping an expression of professional calm on her face that at least didn't look like she had noticed the drool on my chin.

"I'm sorry I missed you coming aboard, sir. Chief

Engineer O'Malley requested a conference with me. I came as soon as I was able to leave engineering."

"Uh," I said. Real smooth. Did she know how great she looked in that skinsuit? She had to, right? "No problem, Commander. Ensign...Stevens," I think I said the right name, "showed me to my quarters. And I've already met some of the crew." No need to tell her about the aggressive and surreal encounter with Jacobs yet, not before I had a better handle on the obvious personnel issues on this horrid little ship.

"Thank you, sir," she said with a hint of a shy smile. That had to be affected; there was no way a woman who looked like *that* could ever really be shy. Then her smile disappeared. "I trust that the crew is being accommodating thus far?"

The way she asked the question, with a mix of trepidation and hopefulness, made me think that she had already guessed or even heard about the encounter with Jacobs. But I decided to play dumb for now. "All in order," I said instead.

"Very good, sir. May I give you a tour of the *Persephone*?" She said the name without the disdain I usually heard it imbued with.

"Of course, Commander," I said reluctantly. "Lead on."

I didn't get much from the tour. The alcohol I'd already imbibed that day had mixed with the shock of the encounter with Jacobs to put my mind into a haze. I couldn't recall later the name of a single person Lin introduced me to or much of what she said about the ship or its capabilities as we roved through its corridors and stopped at the various duty stations.

I pretty much spent the entire time looking over my shoulder for Jacobs, irrationally fearful that the big man would jump out of a hatch at any moment and club me over the head with one of his beefy fists. Any time not spent looking over my shoulder was spent admiring Jessica Lin's exquisitely formed backside as she led the way through the ship. At least there was one bright spot so far in my exile.

I was still staring at her when we stepped through a large hatch into an oven, snapping me out of my trance and making me look around for the first time with some semblance of alert attention.

"And this," Lin said to me, "is engineering. Apologies for the heat, sir. The climate controls down here are a bit temperamental."

"And the blasted ion drive gives off more heat than my mother-in-law's temper," a man's voice said from behind a bank of controls. A broad ruddy face peered around the console, and I found myself looking at the polar opposite of Petty Officer Jacobs. The man now in front of me couldn't have been taller than 160 centimeters, with drab brown hair and pasty white skin blotched with red. But he had laugh lines around his eyes and a smile on his face that instantly made him more likable than the bully giant I had encountered in my quarters earlier.

I threw a quick look around the room to make sure Jacobs wasn't there with us—he wasn't—then turned my attention back to the short man in front of me.

"Sorry, Captain, I'd salute, but I'm trying to fine-tune the reactor's containment field, and if I take my hand off the dial, we may all regret it."

I laughed lightly; I didn't find the man's banter funny, but I knew he would be worried if I didn't at least chuckle. But by the confused look on his face and the semi-horrified look Lin shot my way before she composed her features, I guessed that maybe he *hadn't* been joking after all.

"This is Lieutenant Commander Kelly O'Malley," Lin said, nodding toward the short man.

"Kelly O'Malley?" I asked incredulously.

The man shrugged with one shoulder, hopefully not the one supporting the hand still adjusting the reactor's containment field, and smiled. "I know, huh? Could I be any more Irish?" Then he ducked back behind the control panel ostensibly to keep fiddling with the reactor.

"Just give me a second, Captain," he said in a muffled tone. "And...got it!" He emerged fully now from behind the bank of controls, brushing his hands together as if to remove dust or grease from them. I liked him almost instantly, which is saying something. For the last six months, I'd hated pretty much everyone I'd met.

He reached out one of his hands, and I shook it. "Good to meet you, Cheng. I heard there's a problem with the engine." I tried to keep the hope out of my voice. My orders—at least the little I had read—said we were to leave the station by 0700 tomorrow morning for a long patrol around the outer system. But if the engines were down, we'd have to stay in dock longer, which meant access to the station's bars.

I guess I did a good job hiding my desires because O'Malley smiled and shrugged. "Don't worry, sir. She's a bit temperamental, but these ion engines got a bum rap. They're not so bad once you learn their quirks. We'll be ready to leave dock tomorrow as planned."

Lin beamed proudly at the man's statement, and the smile on her perfect face put one on mine, which O'Malley misread as pleasure at his report. Oh well, that wasn't a bad thing, I supposed.

"Good, Cheng. I, ah, assume there are department reports I can read up on to learn more about the engines and their quirks." Yeah, right; like I was going to read boring engineering reports. But the question made Lin smile again, and I was all for that happening as often as possible.

"Of course, sir. I'll have them sent to your implant."

O'Malley's face took on an expression that reminded me of hope. It mirrored the expression Lin suddenly had as well.

Oh no. These poor fools thought *I* was a source of hope? They'd learn. It also meant their last captain must have been a royal loser. But I still bet I could be worse.

"Captain, it's nearing dinner time. Perhaps we can retire to the wardroom to meet the rest of your officers?" Lin suggested lightly. There went my plans to suggest that she and I have a working dinner *alone*, to help me learn about the ship...and about her.

"Sounds good, Commander," I replied grudgingly.

"If it's all right with you, Captain," O'Malley said with a frown. "I'll stay down here and keep working on the engines so we don't miss our departure time tomorrow. I can have dinner brought down to me."

"Carry on, Cheng," I said with a nod. At least that meant one less interloper to distract me from Jessica Lin.

It took us about five minutes to get back up to officer country, or what passed for it on the *Persephone*. With such a small ship, there weren't the natural divisions of territory you would get on a ship of the line or even a modest size cruiser. The little frigate made my last command, *HMS Lancer*, a battlecruiser, look palatial by comparison.

The wardroom was no exception to that. Space was at a premium on any King's ship, but the small room Lin led me to looked barely big enough to hold the two people waiting there for us. I had no idea where the commander and I would squeeze in, and I had a warm but fleeting mental image of Lin sitting on my lap at the head of the table and feeding me grapes. Carla would have slapped me for being a misogynistic pig. She'd be right, but that didn't stop me from smiling at the fantasy.

The two officers already in the room stood up awkwardly—the table's benches were so close to the bulkheads that they couldn't stand behind them, so they stood uncomfortably bent in the even narrower space between them and the wardroom table—as we entered.

"As you were," I said, more out of habit than out of any genuine care for their comfort. They sat down gratefully anyway.

"Captain Mendoza, allow me to introduce Lieutenant Junior Grade Petra Yesayan," she gestured toward a mousy-looking young woman with dirty blond hair and an anachronistic pair of glasses on her face. "And Lieutenant Senior Grade Richard Ingbar," she nodded toward a slightly pudgy-looking man with a receding hairline and a double chin.

I nodded at both of them. Lin hesitated as if waiting for me to say something. When I didn't, she continued. "Lieutenant Yesayan is our helm officer, and Lieutenant Ingbar is our tactical officer."

The man nodded back at me. "I also double as our sensor officer. Small ship, sir. We all have more than one job."

I nodded back as if I cared.

"And I double as our navigator," chimed in Yesayan in a surprisingly high and squeaky voice—well, maybe not that surprising given that I'd already described her in my head as 'mousy'.

"And you've already met Ensign Stevens," Lin continued. "He's on bridge watch right now and won't be joining us for dinner."

I almost scoffed at that. Bridge watch while *docked*? Sure, regulations demanded it, but I hadn't expected to find a bunch of rule followers on the worst ship in the King's Navy.

I took my seat at the table's head while Lin sat to my right next to Ingbar, and unfortunately, not on my lap. I cleared my throat and asked the first lame question I could think of. "And how long have the two of you been on the *Persephone*?"

Lin frowned in my peripheral vision, and I realized my mistake. As captain, I should have already *known* the answer to that question. It would have been included in the briefing packet attached to my orders. Oh well. Hopefully, they would all just think I was trying to make small talk.

"I've been on the ship for three months," Yesayan answered simply.

"And I've been on the *Phony* for almost a year now," Ingbar said with a small frown. Lin shot him a sharp look that could have powered the ion drive if the reactor ever went down.

"The *Phony*?" I asked, causing Lin's frown to deepen. But I couldn't help myself.

Ingbar shot an apologetic glance at my XO, then shrugged. "Sorry, sir. It's the crew's nickname for *Persephone*. Fitting, too, if I'm not too bold."

I chuckled. Here was the first person I'd encountered on the ship who wasn't either threatening me or trying to make me forget I was on the laughingstock of His Majesty's pointy-ended spear. Of course, Ingbar looked rather old for a lieutenant senior grade, so I'm sure he was just as much of a loser as me, but that might make him easier to deal with.

"It has a ring to it," I admitted.

Lin frowned more fiercely. But it was Yesayan who spoke first. "We've been trying to keep the crew from using it; it's disrespectful. But so far, we haven't managed to stamp it out completely." She threw a look at Ingbar that rivaled the one Lin had given him a few seconds ago. I almost laughed again.

"Well, sometimes it doesn't hurt to let the crew have their fun," I said with a lopsided grin. As I expected, anger flashed on Yesayan's face before she composed herself and nodded once to acknowledge my comment.

Lin shook her head but didn't seem quite as offended as Yesayan.

"In any event," I continued. "Tell me about your departments." It was the question they would be expecting from me. And it launched both junior officers into monologues about their few personnel and systems.

I let them talk while a spacer brought in something that looked like it *might* be dinner. It tasted worse than it looked, but I hadn't eaten since lunch on the transport, and the alcohol I'd had earlier was no help. While I ate, I nodded along and made small sounds of agreement at some parts to make them think I was listening. At one point, I thought Lin might have caught me staring at her a little too closely, but I quickly moved my head as if I'd been panning my gaze around the table and not drooling over her curves again.

All in all, the first dinner in the wardroom wasn't a total disaster. Too bad the rest of the night would be.

CHAPTER 5

Trying to Forget

I'd hoped to dream about Jessica Lin when I hit my bunk that night. But I dreamed about Carla instead, back to the first time I'd seen her after the Bellerophon disaster. In the dream, I arrived home on a fast naval transport, a courtesy extended to a man of my rank, though I'd clearly been summoned back to Prometheus to stand trial for what had happened. People on the transport had treated me a bit oddly, as if they weren't sure what to do with me.

Carla was waiting at the airlock on Home Station One when the transport docked. She ran up to me the second I disembarked, wrapping her arms around me and burying her head in my chest.

"Brad, I'm so glad you're home," she said in a voice that sounded like she meant it.

I knew better. I wasn't coming home after a simple deployment or to get another promotion or even attend another of the endless military balls where her father would beam at his daughter and cast disapproving glances at me.

No, I was coming home because I might be losing my freedom. And I wasn't sure how I felt about that. Part of me resented it, of course. No one *wanted* to be court-martialed and possibly imprisoned. But the other part of me knew I deserved it. After all, my actions had resulted in about five hundred people —five hundred and four, to be exact; all innocent civilians—dead.

I pushed Carla away, refusing to meet her gaze. I said nothing, not trusting my voice, and instead gently moved her aside so I could continue walking down the corridor toward my fate...

I woke up from the dream with the same sense of futility I'd felt when I'd gotten off that transport. Except now, I felt a double sense of frustration. Because that had been the moment when I'd first pushed Carla away...when I'd first made her feel that she was no longer my wife.

Not that I could have done any differently. I didn't deserve her, and I knew it. My biggest regret was that I hadn't pushed her away more directly. What I should have done was file for divorce the second I'd arrived home on Prometheus, freeing her to move on with her life without any guilt or backward glances. After all, there was no way her dear old dad was going to let her stay married to the Butcher of

Bellerophon. I knew it, and she must have known it too.

But instead of doing the brave thing and telling her right then and there it was over, I stayed silent, letting her stew in uncertainty as I turned away from her and never once let her back in. It hadn't even surprised me three months later when I'd found her in bed with Vice Admiral Clarington's son. By then, it was finally clear to her that there was no future with me.

Now I lay awake in my bunk, reliving *that* wonderful moment in my head. Even though I'd pushed Carla away and had even decided that I needed to cut her loose for her own good, it had still hurt to find her in bed with that empty-headed idiot Clarington. Without his daddy's influence, the guy wouldn't have risen to command even a transport. But apparently, a battleship captain who got his post purely through nepotism was still a better option for Carla than a disgraced murderer. I couldn't argue with her logic. Though, seeing her with another man had hurt far more than I ever could have imagined.

It was the worst mental image I retained in a long line of horrible ones from the last six months of my sorry life. And that was saying something! I'd killed a few hundred children, after all.

There was no going back to sleep now. With nothing else to do and needing a distraction, I eyed my footlocker. Getting out of my bunk, I stumbled the two steps over to it, keying it open with my personal code; it took a couple of tries, given the sleep in my eyes.

Once it was open, I reached in and pulled out a bottle. I had almost done this when I'd first returned from dinner in the wardroom. But exhausted from my travels—I never slept all that well on transports —I had exercised a modicum of self-control and gone to bed instead, telling Lin I was not to be disturbed so that I could catch up on reading the myriad of reports she and the other officers had already sent me.

Like I would *ever* read those.

Now, though, sleep fled, and I almost frantically twisted open the top of one of the bottles I'd purchased on the station, a cheap tequila. Not bothering with a glass, I lifted the entire thing to my lips and took a swig. It burned horribly going down, and I almost gagged, but I took another sip afterward and then another. I'd always hated tequila, but the pain was oddly comforting now.

I lost track of the number of swigs I took, but it at least helped me mostly forget the image of Carla in bed with Clarington.

I have no idea when or how long I passed out, but I woke up to find myself on the floor of my cabin, lying in something wet. I groaned when I saw the tipped-over tequila bottle, the contents I hadn't drunk all over the floor near my bunk and soaking into my skinsuit. There was a little vomit mixed in as well. That bottle, along with the other two I'd brought aboard, needed to last me for the entirety of the three-week patrol me and the *Phony* were set to embark on in the morning. But just like that, a third of my liquor supply was gone.

Suddenly, a pair of shoes appeared in front of my face. My first panicked thought was that Lin had found me passed out in a pool of alcohol and puke. That would surely hurt my chances with her. But even in my fogged and drunken state, I recognized the big feet of a man. Wincing at the pain it caused in my neck, I peered upward to see an older salt with graying hair and an enlisted man's uniform frowning down at me.

"Who the…?" I started to ask, but a fit of coughing cut it off.

"Sir, I'm Warrant Officer Hoag," the intruder said in a deep baritone voice. "Ship's supply officer…and your steward."

"My what?" I knew what he'd said. But ships the size of *Persephone* usually didn't warrant a warrant officer *or* a steward. 'Warrant a warrant officer.' I might have laughed at my own internal play on words if my brain weren't so foggy.

"Your steward, Captain Mendoza," the man said with a pronounced grimace. "I'm sorry I wasn't on board when you first arrived. I was securing the last of our supplies from Gerson Station Control, and I just returned to the ship a few hours ago. I was coming to get you for breakfast, but you didn't answer my knock."

"Well…" I started. But then I trailed off; I really had no idea what I was about to say. And I was still lying on the ground, not my preferred position from which to say anything pithy.

"Sir, we're due to leave dock in a little over an hour. With all due respect," funny how people who said that usually didn't say it with even a modicum of actual respect, "we need to get you cleaned up and on the bridge."

I didn't argue. I was too wasted to do so. Instead, I let Hoag lift me off the floor and help me into my personal head, where I promptly vomited again, missing the head but spraying his shoes quite liberally. Minutes later, I was naked in the tiny shower, with no memory of how I'd gotten undressed.

Shortly after that, I was drinking a cup of the blackest, strongest coffee I'd ever tasted, all under the watchful and blatantly judgmental eye of Warrant Officer Hoag.

He said little else to me that I can recall. But somewhere around my third cup of coffee, I remembered to feel at least mildly embarrassed for the state he'd found me in. I even mumbled an apology for throwing up on his shoes.

Hoag left after that and returned a few minutes later with a plate of breakfast. Given how terrible dinner had been the night before, I was loath to even try anything on my plate, but my new steward slash overseer wouldn't let me get away with skipping breakfast. Using few words but many stern looks, he made it clear I was expected to eat *everything* on my plate.

So, I did. And it was shockingly good. Maybe they'd executed the cook who had dared to serve us the slop for dinner last night and somehow replaced him with a magical unicorn who used the black arts to turn the Navy's powdered eggs into something that tasted better even than the real thing. Either way, I didn't care. I'd shoot the other cook myself if it paved the way for whoever had prepared this breakfast to take over all cooking duties on the *Phony*.

Before I knew it, I had cleaned the plate. Then I barely made it to the head before I threw up again. Lovely.

CHAPTER 6

Something is Seriously Wrong Here

I groaned inwardly as I stood on the bridge of my new command, looking forlornly at the tiny space with only four duty stations in addition to my command chair. I'd once served as the tactical officer on the expansive bridge of a Hera-class fleet carrier. Persephone's entire bridge could have fit into just the space I'd had for my tactical station there.

And it was kind of dirty. Dust covered some of the controls, and there was an unknown grease on one arm of my chair and a weird-looking stain on the floor next to it. I saw Commander Lin blush when she noticed me studying it.

Hoag had gotten me mostly sober and on the bridge before the scheduled time for us to depart the station. But semi-sober didn't mean free of a massive migraine that had me squinting at the bright lights on the bridge.

"XO, tell Gerson Control we are retracting docking clamps and moving away on thruster power."

Lin acknowledged my command—I'd learned she included comms officer amongst her many duties on the bridge—and crisply relayed the message.

"Helm, fire port thrusters at ten percent," I commanded, and Yesayan confirmed the order after a slight hesitation. I knew what was bothering her. Ten percent power was a bit much for an undocking procedure; usually, five percent was more than enough to move a ship far enough away from a station to light up its main drive. But I'd ordered ten percent *because* I knew it would bother Yesayan. I had so few joys left in life.

"Captain, message from Gerson Control," Lin said with a weird measure of excitement in her voice. "Happy hunting, *Persephone*."

I wanted to snicker. It was the traditional send-off for a ship leaving station, and I had heard it hundreds of times before. But it suddenly struck me as ridiculous in this situation. First of all, a piece of junk like *Persephone* wasn't going to be *hunting* anyone. The best we could do if we encountered trouble was to call in reinforcements and run the other way while we hoped the finicky ion drive didn't crap out on us. And second of all, there would be nothing *happy* about this voyage.

But I sensed that actually laughing out loud would break Lin. She looked so eager and shiny about leaving port that I could almost believe she *wanted* a dull patrol of the outer system. But whether it was affected or not, she looked spectacular while she sat at her station and watched the forward viewscreen, so I decided just to enjoy it and not burst her bubble.

"Engineering," I called, the bridge's AI automatically relaying my voice down to the ship's depths. "Is that ion drive ready for me, Cheng?"

"Yes, sir!" came the overly enthusiastic reply from O'Malley, and I couldn't help but shake my head slightly. "Ready when you need her, Captain."

Fine, even if I had been praying that we'd have a last-minute malfunction that would keep us on station for another day or two. Heck, if I was lucky, we would have had a catastrophic failure that would have put us in dry dock for the next three months. But apparently, I was cursed with a good chief engineer or just the worst luck of any captain in the history of the King's Navy.

Either way, we were due for our date with some random dust cloud out past Gerson's asteroid belt. Maybe we'd see smugglers if we were really lucky. Or unlucky, from my point of view.

"Very well. Helm, prepare to go to one-third power on the main drive," I said reluctantly.

Lin twitched at her station as if I'd slapped her. "Uh, sir. Don't you think you should say a few words to the crew before we light up the main drive? Maybe tell them our orders...or introduce yourself."

Ugh. Lin may be hotter than most movie stars I'd ever seen, but she was starting to get a little annoying.

"Oh, of course," I answered lamely. "Open a ship-wide channel, please, XO."

She nodded and motioned to me that it was done. I hesitated, then started talking.

"Ladies and gentlemen, this is Captain Brad Mendoza speaking. I have taken command of *His Majesty's Ship Persephone* as of..." I checked my implant, "1700 hours yesterday. Our orders are to embark on a routine patrol of the outer system for the next three weeks, after which we will return to Gerson Station for resupply and redeployment. That is all."

I motioned for Lin to cut the channel. She did so, but I could see from her face that she was disappointed in me. What had she been expecting, some grand speech? As if it would mean anything to the screwups on *this* ship. That thought quickly made me picture the massive Jacobs laughing at any speech I did try and make. I promptly thrust that image aside and focused back on my XO. She was still looking at me and frowning.

Oh well. I couldn't please everyone. Maybe she would want to talk about it later, in private, maybe in my quarters.

That mental image I did my best to keep around, all the way to the outer system.

Dinner that evening was significantly better than it had been the night before. I learned that Hoag was normally the cook on *Persephone* but that he'd been gone last night, as he'd told me, securing the ship's final supplies. That had left a spacer second class to cook dinner in his absence, and the results had been abysmal. But now that Hoag was back, I had to admit that this voyage might have a bright spot, apart from Lin's extraordinary derriere. My new steward was an excellent cook, somehow turning even boring and semi-disgusting naval rations into something that wasn't just edible but actually enjoyable.

Lin was silent at dinner. Apparently, my less-than-inspirational speech when we'd left station had upset her more than I'd counted on. She wouldn't even meet my gaze.

Yesayan, on the other hand, was glaring at me. I'd pegged her right for a rules stickler, and my little stunt overpowering the thrusters to undock had her tied in knots. At least I'd been able to crush the hope they'd both had in me; better to set expectations early.

I was making friends all over the place. Luckily, O'Malley joined us tonight, along with Ensign Whats-His-Name—the dumb one who seemed happy to be on the *Phony*. Ingbar had the bridge watch. So, the gregarious chief engineer did most of the talking, prattling on about some fine-tune adjustments he was making to the ship's artificial gravity. Something about gaining a few extra g's of acceleration on the upper end with better inertial dampening. I tried to pay attention; I really did. But it had been a while since I'd had to keep to a fixed schedule. Drinking myself into oblivion in the months since my court martial hadn't exactly required me to be up at a particular time in the morning.

So, I barely made it through dinner without falling asleep face-first in my pasta. Which would have been a shame. Hoag had somehow gotten his hands on *fresh* tomatoes to use in the sauce. Where he got those on an orbital station was beyond me, but I wasn't going to argue with the man's results.

Dinner finally ended, and I stood up and made a weak excuse about paperwork I needed to get done. There *was* paperwork—it was an eternal struggle for ship commanders to keep ahead of the virtual piles of it—but I had no intention of actually doing any of it. I just desperately needed to sleep.

Unfortunately, my XO had other ideas. Lin followed me out of the wardroom, and I was halfway back to my quarters before I realized she was right behind me. Turning to face her, I tried not to let my exhaustion and frustration show. I'd daydreamed of her following me back to my cabin, but by the look on her face, this was *not* the circumstance I'd been fantasizing about.

"Yes, Commander?" I prompted, raising my

eyebrows both to look inquisitive and to keep my eyes open.

She stopped in her tracks, looking momentarily abashed but then visibly squaring her shoulders and looking me in the eye. "Sir, I wonder if you and I might talk? In private?"

Inwardly I sighed. But outwardly, I nodded. "Of course, Commander. Let's use my office."

I thought an impromptu confrontation with Lin would be the worst of my problems that night, but just before we reached my quarters, we ran into Petty Officer Jacobs.

I must admit that in the last day since taking command, I had largely managed to irrationally convince myself that I wouldn't often run into the man on the ship. Ridiculous—there were only twenty-four of us on the entire *Persephone*, after all. This wasn't a battleship with its crew of two thousand or even my old battlecruiser with its crew of eight hundred. This was a tiny frigate, and the only thing smaller than the crew was the space for that crew. We were all literally living on top of each other.

Jacobs was coming down the corridor in one direction as Lin and I approached from the other. Upon seeing us, he sneered and seemed to square his shoulders to take up *more* of the narrow corridor. I was suddenly left with two undesirable options. I could either make way for him by pressing myself against the corridor wall—as the ship's commander, that would be directly against protocol and a terrible precedent to set. Or I could meet him, engage in a contest of wills, and see if I could get him to make way. If he did, I would win a small victory. If he didn't, things could escalate very quickly.

I have to admit I almost immediately settled on the first option. Better to lose a little face than escalate things, I guess. But then I happened to glance back at Lin and saw that she had cast her eyes down to the deck and turned a shade or two whiter. She had gone from the posture of a somewhat confident —or, at least, angry—and beautiful woman to one very reminiscent of a dog I'd once seen whose owner regularly beat it. And seeing that transformation made my blood suddenly boil.

In the last six months, I had lost virtually all of my self-respect. But seeing a pretty girl threatened still managed to ignite some righteous indignation in me. I suppose it was the last little part of my honor I hadn't managed to snuff out.

"Ah, Mr. Jacobs," I said firmly as the man approached. His sneer didn't go away. "I'd hoped to run into you." Now he looked confused but managed to keep a disdainful grin that no longer reached his eyes.

"What of it, Mendoza?" he asked belligerently. It was an odd response. What of what? But I rolled with it.

"Mr. Jacobs, you will address me as 'Captain' or 'Sir' as long as I am your commanding officer. That aside, your behavior in my cabin yesterday was completely unacceptable. You are to report to the mess at 0400 tomorrow morning to clean it, top to bottom. I *will* be inspecting it."

He faltered for a second; then, his face turned red.

"You can't..." he started to say, but I cut him off.

"I can, and I will, Mr. Jacobs. And unless you'd like this to become a daily chore for you, you will carefully watch your next words." I didn't know I still had that in me, but old command habits apparently don't go away completely just because said commander turns into a worthless screwup with no self-respect or future.

He frowned, but I could tell he was considering all the angles. I had reached him now, and we stood in the corridor squared off with each other, less than a meter separating me from those vice-like hands and forearms that could surely crush the life out of me. Luckily for me, he chose not to argue. Then he did something that surprised me. He gave way, moving to the side of the corridor with his back pressed to the bulkhead so we could pass, which I did, careful not to meet his hateful gaze.

I had moved past him and heard Lin's footsteps behind me. Then I heard something else that was completely out of place in the corridor of a warship. It sounded like a smack. But it wasn't the sound of someone hitting a bulkhead as they tried to move around another person in a corridor; it was a sound that even my foggy brain almost instantly identified as a hand against cloth-covered skin, specifically in a fattier part of someone's body.

I whirled, and by the look on Lin's face, I knew my impression was accurate. Jacobs had slapped Lin on the butt when she'd passed him! I opened my mouth to reprimand him, my anger rising, but then I saw the pleading look in Lin's eyes and shut my mouth just as quickly. Jacobs just leered at her from behind.

I turned and proceeded the remaining distance to my quarters, my XO following behind still like a beaten dog. Something was seriously wrong on this ship! And I was going to find out what.

CHAPTER 7

So Many Mistakes

We got into the outer office in my quarters, and the hatch shut behind us. I didn't even take my seat or invite Lin to take one; I whirled and regarded her from just half a meter away—that was all the standing room there was in the small space.

"OK, Commander," I said. "Spill it. Just what is going on between you and P.O. Jacobs?"

She looked down, refusing to meet my gaze. For a long moment, she said nothing. Then she shook her head. "Nothing, sir. Just a personal matter. It's none of your concern."

It was my turn to shake my head. "*Everything* that happens on this ship is my concern, Commander Lin."

That was a mistake. She looked up at me now, a fire in her eyes and a hard set to her mouth. "Really, sir?

Permission to speak freely?"

"Granted." My second mistake.

"With all due respect..." Again, how come people only use those words when no actual respect is implied? "...how can you say that when you don't seem to care about *anything* happening on this ship? Do you realize you called Ensign Stevens by the wrong name three times at dinner tonight? Or that the punishment duty you just gave Jacobs isn't a punishment for him at all? That mess will be sparkling clean by the time you inspect it, but I guarantee Jacobs himself won't be the one to clean it."

I wanted to stop her there and dig into that, but I didn't speak up fast enough and missed my opening. My third mistake. She continued.

"You don't seem to care about yourself or anyone else on this ship. You think I couldn't smell the alcohol on your breath this morning on the bridge? And if I smelled it, so did the other officers. I realize you may not respect yourself, but please do us the courtesy of respecting this ship and its crew."

"Are you done?" I asked the question with a lot more anger in my tone than I'd intended. My fourth mistake.

"Yes, sir!" She said it with such vehemence that it momentarily left me speechless.

When I found my voice, it lacked its prior

confidence. "He smacked you in the hallway, didn't he?"

She grimaced, confirming it for me. "Again, sir. It's a personal matter. I will handle it."

I raised an eyebrow. Not everyone can raise just one, you know. I'd always been proud that I could do it quite well. "Commander, that's a major breach of protocol. Enough for a court martial."

"You would know," she muttered under her breath, but we were close enough for me to hear it. I chose to ignore it. Probably the first thing I'd done right in this entire terrible conversation.

"Commander Lin. Is there something going on between you and P.O. Jacobs? Some sort of romantic entanglement?" Ugh. My fifth mistake. By the anger and shame that flashed across her face, I'd hit the nail on the head. But she violently shook her head.

"Sir. There is nothing you need to concern yourself with."

"Really, Lin? *Him*?" Uh-oh. Sixth and, by far, my biggest mistake, and I knew it as soon as the words left my mouth.

Her face turned even harder, and she took a step forward, forcing her to look up at a sharper angle right into my eyes. "What, sir? Mad because it's not you? Note from a woman subordinate: you've spent more time looking at my chest and butt than my face since you came aboard, so you can't be one to talk.

Who I choose to get…entangled with is none of your business!"

That wasn't true, strictly speaking. It was a major breach of naval regulations for Lin to be romantically involved with *any* subordinate, including P.O. Jacobs. That I'd been hoping forlornly for the same kind of relationship with her myself —an even bigger breach of regulations given my position as captain and hers as my XO—was beside the point right now. But how to tell her that? I was so shocked by her brazen calling out of my leering gaze that I was left speechless. And extremely embarrassed on top of that.

I mean, I suppose that it shouldn't have surprised me that a woman can tell when a man is undressing her with his eyes. But I'd never been called out on it before, so guess I'd fooled myself into thinking that the women I looked at that way didn't notice or that perhaps I was good enough at hiding it that they never caught on. And I'd managed to largely stop doing it at all after I'd met Carla, at least with women other than her.

But apparently, I was wrong. And I'd managed to turn what was actually a semi-well-meaning intervention—by the way Jacobs had made her cower in the corridor, it was clear that any relationship between Lin and the brute was not weighted in her favor—into an indictment of my own actions.

That hurt. No good deed goes unpunished, I suppose. But Lin was right; I'd lost any moral high ground from which to judge her actions.

She didn't wait for me to respond or even to dismiss her. She spun on one foot, threw the hatch open, and stormed out of my office and into the corridor, slamming the hatch behind her.

I caught myself watching her rear end as she did so. If I could have punched myself out, I would have done so in that moment.

CHAPTER 8

The Detour

"Captain, we're on station at the first waypoint," Lt. Yesayan said from the helm.

I'd managed not to come onto the bridge this morning smelling of alcohol. Not because I hadn't drunk myself into oblivion the night before. I was quickly draining my supply of liquor. I imagined that, on a ship with *Persephone's* reputation, the enlisted spacers probably had a hidden still somewhere. But the last person they were likely to want to share its output with would be their captain. It was going to be a serious problem. Bad things happened to me when I didn't drink.

No, I didn't smell like alcohol this morning because I'd remembered to take one of the anti-hangover pills I'd brought onboard in my footlocker. Technology had come a long way in the thousands of years since man had first invented alcohol and drunkenness, and those pills were probably my favorite invention of that whole period. Not only did they do a fairly good job of driving away the headache and nausea that were common after a bender, but they also managed to mask the stench on one's breath, but only if I remembered to take them *before* I started drinking.

I'd also shaved this morning for the first time since coming on board. But that hadn't been my idea. Hoag had made it clear when he'd woken me up that if I didn't shave myself, he would do the honors... with a straight razor he kept soaking in pure rubbing alcohol. I think he mentioned using salt as an aftershave as well. I knew he was messing with me —maybe—but it was enough to make me elect to do my own shaving.

The man had even managed to press my uniform. I was almost insulted. It took a lot of work to make a *skin*suit look rumpled and wrinkly. I was mildly proud of my capabilities in that area until Hoag ruined my streak.

"Thank you, Lieutenant," I responded to Yesayan. My words only slurred a little; the stupid pills didn't take care of that little problem as well as I thought they should. "Lieutenant Ingbar..." Had I gotten the name right? "Please conduct a full scan of the area, protocol four. Once done, we will move to the second waypoint."

Boring. Seriously, nothing was more tedious than

an outer system patrol. Space was *huge*. And the chances of us happening to stumble upon a pirate or smuggler in the vast expanse of an outer star system weren't just low; they were virtually nonexistent. The only thing an outer system patrol was really good for, everyone knew, was to show the flag. The idea was that the mere presence of a warship on patrol would send the pirates and smugglers scurrying away with their tails between their legs.

I'd dealt with a few pirates and smugglers in my time. They *weren't* the type to be worried about the infinitesimally small probability that a single warship on patrol would see them, much less be in a position to catch them. And even if they were, I couldn't imagine *anyone* being the least bit intimidated by the *Phony*.

"Captain, may I suggest we randomize our pattern?" It was the first thing Lin had said to me in the three hours since we'd all been on the bridge for the day watch. Even as she said it, she didn't look over at me. I'd been careful to keep my eyes off of her, mostly. It was far more challenging than it should have been. I was pretty sure that at some point in my life, I'd had far more self-control than this. After all, I'd once been a happily married and entirely faithful husband.

But a lot can happen to you after you kill five hundred innocent civilians and drive your wife into the arms of another man.

"Explain, Commander," I prompted. It wasn't unheard of for a warship to vary its patrol pattern away from the fixed waypoints and timings, but it also wasn't the norm.

Lin didn't respond immediately. I wasn't looking over at her. I'd found a spot of discoloration on the opposite bridge bulkhead that I had spent a large chunk of the morning studying intently for that very reason. I was really scrutinizing it now. It kind of looked like a jellyfish.

"Sir," she finally said, her voice brimming with uncertainty. "I have no confirmation of this, but there have been...rumors that our patrol patterns have been leaking out of Gerson Station."

Now I *did* look over at her, but I was proud of myself that my entire focus was on her face—her perfect face with those stunning eyes and plump lips...

I literally shook myself in my seat, like a dog, drawing a sharp look from Yesayan. Lin ignored me. Ingbar was either too busy doing his sensor sweep, or he was playing a game with his implant. Either was equally likely.

"That's quite an accusation, Commander," I said. "Any evidence to back it up?"

She finally looked over at me, frowning, and for a moment, I thought she might back down and retract her suggestion. But she seemed to find a modicum of inner strength instead. "No, sir. At least none worth sharing. But even the rumor makes me think we should take precautions. If we vary our pattern even a little, we might catch whoever is trying to use the information to get through our patrol cordon."

Unlikely. We could completely randomize our pattern and still have almost no chance of seeing anyone. Or...

"Helm," I addressed Yesayan. "If someone knew our patrol pattern and schedule and wanted to enter or leave the system in the furthest possible place from where we are *supposed* to be, while also avoiding other patrols and the planetary sensor network, where would they go?"

I could see the woman's eyes go out of focus as she interfaced with her implant. It only took a few moments before she refocused and looked over at me.

"There are three possibilities, Captain," she said, her squeaky voice somehow crisp and professional. How did *she* end up on the *Phony*? I had my suspicions, but that's all they were. "First option is an approach between Hellguard and Heavengate." Those were the names of two gas giants in the system. I quickly checked my own implant and saw that they were at one of the closest approaches to each other in their respective orbits. A ship approaching the system between the two of them would be able to use their bulks to mask its sensor signature from a good portion of the system's scanners.

"Second option would be to approach from the leeward side of Gerson itself." That made sense and was pretty standard. Approaching from the 'leeward' side of the system's star would put that star's heat and bright fury between the approaching ship and the sensors of the one inhabited planet in the system, Gerson 3. Funny that they gave the creative names to the gas giants and not to the actual settled world.

"And the third?"

Yesayan hesitated as if she were having second thoughts about sharing her conclusions with me. But then she continued. "Well, sir. If it were me, I'd approach straight through waypoint eight."

I frowned. "And why is that?" Something nagged at my sleep-deprived and still somewhat drunk mind. I felt like I should *know* the answer to my own question—that I *would* have known it just six months ago—but it wasn't coming to me now.

"Sir," she responded. "When most patrol ships randomize their patterns, they still follow the same general direction around the system. Waypoint eight is a quarter of the way around the system from where we are now. And we're not scheduled to be there for another two and a half weeks; it's the last stop on this patrol pattern. *If* we're dealing with someone who has our schedule, what better way to ensure we won't be in their way than by choosing the place where they *know* we won't be now? But because we *will* be there later, we're likely to discount it in our after-patrol reports. So, it means they can continue to use that route because it would tacitly be declared 'secure' by system command."

She'd only done a passable job of explaining herself. Too many words and the circular reasoning made my head spin. But she also made sense, even to my sluggish brain. I thought that maybe I'd misjudged my helmsman and navigator. I'd pegged her as a rule-following stickler, but she was showing some creative thinking right now that surprised me.

"Commander Lin, your recommendation?"

Lin looked surprised. Had the last captain—I suddenly realized I'd never even bothered to learn the previous captain's name—never asked her for her opinion? Or was she just surprised that *I* was asking for it?

"Sir," she hesitated only briefly, "I think we should proceed to waypoint eight."

I shrugged. "Ok."

Both of the women looked at me with shocked expressions. And I was almost certain at this point that Ingbar *was* playing a game on his implant; I'm not even sure he knew we were having a conversation.

"Finish up the scan here and then proceed to waypoint eight, three-quarters speed." That would put us at the other waypoint, which was pretty far away, in oh... Never mind. One of the first skills I lost when I became a drunken failure and murderer was the ability to do math in my head. Luckily, Yesayan apparently still remembered how to do it, or she cheated and used her implant.

"Yes, sir. At that speed, we will arrive at waypoint eight in thirty-one point-five hours."

"Very well." I stood up from my chair. "I'm going to catch up on some administrative items. Commander Lin, you have the conn."

I wasn't actually going to go do paperwork, but a sandwich sounded pretty good right about then.

CHAPTER 9

A Terrible Discovery

I'd almost forgotten about the punishment I'd inflicted on Jacobs the day before, but I was hungry, and thinking about the mess reminded me that the man was supposed to have cleaned it. I decided to kill two birds with one stone and made my way there.

When I arrived, Jacobs wasn't there, but four spacers were. I vaguely remembered seeing one of them somewhere before on the ship, but the other three were new faces to me. All four stood in surprise when I entered the mess. Technically, this area was for the enlisted men and women. My being here bordered on a breach of protocol, though more so of tradition than any actual regulation. The enlisted spacers needed a place they could go where their captain wouldn't be looking over their shoulders.

"As you were," I waved them all down. They sat hesitantly, not taking their eyes off me.

Hoag appeared out of nowhere, wiping his hands on a towel and giving me a look that clearly conveyed that *he* wasn't pleased to have me there and that he recognized the breach I'd worried about. But whatever; it was my stupid ship.

"Chief," I nodded to him. "I asked Petty Officer Jacobs to clean the mess this morning." I looked around. The room *looked* pretty clean, but never having seen it before, I had no reference point to know if it was always like this or cleaner than usual.

"Aye, sir," Hoag responded. "The mess was cleaned this morning."

The way he said it recalled to me Lin's comment from the night before.

"Chief, did Mr. Jacobs clean the mess as ordered?"

Hoag didn't respond immediately but glanced over at the four enlisted men who were trying very hard to listen to every word without *looking* like they were listening to every word.

"Sir," he said slowly. "It is my understanding that Petty Officer Jacobs' duties required him to be elsewhere this morning, so he delegated the duty of mess cleanup."

I was afraid of that, and I couldn't say that Lin hadn't warned me. Of course, *delegating* a disciplinary duty like Jacobs had done was grounds for a charge of insubordination. Technically, I could now throw him in the brig. But the expression on Hoag's face and the way his shoulders tensed, along with the anticipatory smiles I saw on the faces of two of the enlisted men at the nearby table, threw up warning signs that could even get through my special brand of stupidity. There was something at play here that I wasn't fully aware of.

"Very well, Chief," I said. "I am glad to hear the mess was cleaned. I will be sure to...extend my thanks to Mr. Jacobs for his work."

Hoag's shoulders visibly relaxed, and one of the two smiling enlisted men smirked.

Just what was happening on this Crown-forsaken ship? Did I want to know? Did I *care* to know? I wasn't sure.

But I was sure that I was hungry. So, I asked Hoag to make me a sandwich. I have no idea how that man made dehydrated turkey and cheese taste so good, but I was seriously thinking that if things didn't work out with Lin, maybe I could marry my steward. At least then I'd never go hungry. I took the food and headed back to my cabin.

The surreal experience with Lin and Jacobs the night before, along with the strange energy of the enlisted mess, finally convinced me it was time to actually read the personnel files that had come attached to my orders. Heck, maybe it was even time to read my *orders* in their entirety.

I started there and was interested to find that my orders were pretty explicit on not only the waypoints I was supposed to patrol but the order and timing in which I was supposed to patrol them. These weren't part of the original orders but had been appended by Captain Wainwright. I'd actually never seen patrol orders that gave so little latitude, and that technically meant that *I* was now insubordinate for following Lin's recommendation to vary our pattern.

Oh well, what were they going to do to me, assign me to the *Persephone*?

But it did make me think that maybe there was something to Lin's concerns about leaks. If all the patrol orders in this system were so strict, anyone with access to those orders could pretty much come and go as they pleased without risking entanglements with the Navy. It almost made me curious.

Next, I read the personnel files. Delaying the inevitable foray into Jacobs', I decided to go by descending order of rank. I thought that would mean starting with Lin, but O'Malley was actually senior to her by date of promotion by almost two years.

His file was boring. He'd done little of note, either positive or negative, in almost twelve years of naval service post-Academy. Reading his file actually put me to sleep for a little while.

When I woke up, Lin's file was next. Early on in reading it, I was confused by why she was on

Persephone in the first place. She had high marks in the academy, scoring well in both command potential and tactical capabilities. She'd served with distinction on the battleship *HMS Hood* for her noob cruise just after graduation.

She'd been promoted quickly from ensign to lieutenant and had served in the Combat Information Center (CIC) of *HMS Faraday*, a heavy cruiser, where she had seen actual combat against pirates in the Ophelia system.

Her third assignment had been as a tactical officer on the destroyer *HMS Ordney*, where she'd also been promoted to lieutenant senior grade, a full year ahead of the normal schedule. But then, abruptly, her rise to the top had halted.

For reasons that had been redacted from her file, even for me, she'd been transferred from *Ordney* to a station desk job in the Lightman system. She'd stayed there for two full years, an unheard-of amount of time on desk duty for any officer worth their salt. She'd returned to combat duty on *HMS Ulysses*, another destroyer, where she'd eventually been promoted to lieutenant commander. But as far as I could tell, that promotion had been based not on merit but on simple tenure. She'd reached enough years as a lieutenant senior grade that naval regulations and tradition demanded she either be promoted or drummed out. The powers that be had chosen promotion but then almost immediately transferred her to *Persephone*. She'd been on the dead-end ship now for almost a year and a half.

What had she done on *Ordney* that had halted her career advancement so drastically? And why had it been scrubbed from her file?

Before I could wonder too much at the question, my implant pinged me. It had found supplemental files on Lin in the previous captain's personal logs on *Persephone*. As the new captain, I was granted access to those files by default. Did I want to amend those to her record?

I accepted the prompt, and the first thing that popped up was a video file. My implant asked if I wanted to play it, and I accepted again.

I had picked up a cup of coffee as the video started to play. I dropped it pretty quickly, spilling it all over the floor of my cabin but barely noticing.

I won't describe the video. I wish *I* hadn't had to watch it, but I had to be absolutely sure what I was seeing. Even so, I had my implant scan forward several times to avoid some of the more sordid details.

Needless to say, I now had ironclad proof that Jessica Lin was sleeping with Petty Officer Jacobs. And from everything I could tell, it *wasn't* consensual.

And it wasn't just Jacobs. My implant had helpfully supplied a second video, which showed much the same with another man I had never seen, but whom my implant helpfully identified as Commander

Yancy Jessup, *Persephone's* former captain.

For some reason I couldn't fathom, Jessica Lin had been assaulted by both men, and I had the proof. And as more video files popped up to attach to her file, it became apparent it hadn't been a one-time thing.

I may be a mass murderer, but in my humble opinion, this constituted another level entirely of pure evil. And even in my twisted and broken sense of morality, it was shocking in the extreme. My first inclination was to immediately throw Jacobs in the brig and then send a message to Wainwright to have the Navy find and arrest Jessup wherever he might be. But I stopped myself, fighting to bring my rising anger under control. Because I knew that something like this needed to be approached with a certain measure of caution.

The admiralty may try and sweep it under the rug, and they certainly didn't put it on recruiting posters, but sexual harassment and even rape of this kind was a very real problem in the Promethean Navy. I imagine it had been in every military institution for thousands of years, even back when naval ships had traveled exclusively on water. Honestly, I wasn't sure I even believed those legends; why restrict a ship to only be able to move on water?

I'd been peripherally involved in two prior cases of rape. One had been pretty clear-cut. A commanding officer had used his position to take advantage of a young female lieutenant on his ship, threatening her with a poor performance review if she didn't go along. Scared, she had acquiesced. A friend and fellow junior officer had blown the whistle. The captain had been court-martialed and sent to the stockade. But the lieutenant had resigned her commission in shame; the rumor mill of the Navy was often far worse than any legal penalties. So even though the captain had been the one found guilty, the poor woman had suffered in probably greater measure.

I knew about that particular case only from the news stories and because I'd had a friend on the same ship who had given me some extra details. It had all horrified me.

The other case had been less clean, if the first could even be called that. I had actually served on the court martial panel for this one, as its most junior member. An ensign had been raped by a chief warrant officer on her first post-academy cruise. He'd been drunk and had accosted and assaulted her on a space station when they were both on liberty. She had immediately reported it, putting her trust in the system that she believed would protect her.

The system had failed her tragically.

It had been her word against his. And his story had been that *she* had forced herself on him and demanded that he go along or face disciplinary action. She was technically his commanding officer, even though no ensign with half a brain would ever dream of giving an order to a chief warrant officer, and that automatically cast suspicion on her. Still, things should have gone her way, and I had argued vehemently in the court that the chief be convicted of all charges and dishonorably discharged with a recommendation of the maximum prison sentence.

But then politics had intervened. The warrant officer came from a family that was very well-connected in the Promethean Navy. In the end, the rest of the panel sided with him, and the woman had actually been convicted of the crime for which she'd been the victim. It was a travesty of justice and had been the first time in my naval career that I had been ashamed to wear the uniform. When she had killed herself less than a year later, I had written my resignation letter, and only Carla and my then-father-in-law Terrible Oliphant had stopped me from following through with it.

Even then, had the military judge not put the court members under a gag order, I would have taken the fight to the press. I still almost did but chickened out at the last moment. I justified my silence by telling myself I could do more to change the system from within the Navy and that getting myself discharged would help no one, including the dead woman.

It turns out that even back then, I was cowardly scum and just didn't know it.

So now, I was in a quandary. To me, the

video evidence of Lin's abuse was extremely unambiguous. But none of the videos had sound —part of me was extremely grateful for that— and so I was largely making my judgment off of facial expressions and body language, which I thought made it clear that Lin hadn't been a willing participant in the encounters. But I'd seen good defense attorneys twist evidence like that around pretty handily. The experience with the unfortunate ensign whose career and life I had failed to save as a member of the court had taught me not to take anything for granted when it came to situations like this.

Plus, there was the strangely confident behavior of Jacobs himself. A man who would storm into his new captain's quarters and tell him off on day one and then smack his XO's butt in front of the same captain wasn't a man who feared being caught. He must have *something* he felt would keep him out of trouble and out of the brig. But what?

I was about to open up Jacobs' file and find out, but I couldn't bring myself to do it. The *last* thing I wanted right now was to study more about that man, especially after what I'd just seen. I told myself I'd get to it later.

Instead, I went to my footlocker and pulled out one of the bottles still stashed there. It was still the early afternoon, but now there were new things that I needed to forget.

CHAPTER 10

Contact!

We had just arrived on station at waypoint eight, over a day later, and I was having an incredibly hard time not looking at Jessica Lin. Except it was for very different reasons than before. Now, when I saw her perfect features, all I could see in my mind was the abuse she'd sustained at the hands of at least two different men. If I could have wiped those videos from my memory, and not just my implant, I would have done so in a heartbeat. But even the alcohol wasn't obliging me in that respect.

My guilt was overwhelming, as was my shame. Not just for what I'd seen done to her but for the fact that I had been leering at her almost nonstop since boarding *Persephone*. It made me feel just as dirty as the men who had raped her. I had already known I was a good-for-nothing loser, but I felt I had now sunk even lower.

Beyond the obvious, one other thing bothered me about those videos. I'd only known Lieutenant Commander Jessica Lin for a short time, but she didn't strike me as the type of woman that would *let* those types of things happen to her. Despite some of her timidity on the bridge and with her fellow officers, she'd boldly called me out on my own leering looks at her. The type of woman who would call out her *captain* for inappropriate looks didn't strike me as the type who would let herself be abused by a man under *her* command, even if her former captain was involved.

It just didn't add up. It was like I was seeing two different people. There was a strong and direct woman who had called me on my crap, contrasted with the beaten down woman who had looked like a dog about to be hit in front of Petty Officer Jacobs in the corridor. And somewhere in the middle was the timid woman who had still had the courage to suggest the change to our patrol pattern.

I had rehearsed and discarded dozens of different ways to broach the topic with her. None of them felt even close to right. I found myself desperately wishing Carla was there so I could get a woman's perspective, but alas, I was on my own.

"Sir, beginning sensor sweep," Ingbar said lazily from the tactical station. I still hadn't been able to force myself to read Jacobs' file, but I had, after waking from my bender, read Ingbar's and Yesayan's, mostly as a way to distract myself from the terrible things I'd learned about Lin.

Ingbar's had been more of what I'd expected to see for an officer assigned to *Persephone*. Low marks at the Academy, a lackluster service record afterward, and his promotions only coming for time-in-rank, never for performance or merit.

He was a dead weight on His Majesty's Navy. Pretty much like I'd become, though without the killing of hundreds of innocents.

Yesayan's record was a bit better, but at least some of my initial assessment about her had been right. She'd gotten good grades at the Academy and even had some merit awards since. But every one of her commanding officers had arranged to have her transferred as soon as they could justify it. Several of them cited issues of 'cultural fit'. One was blunter: 'She is the most frustrating junior officer I have ever served with'. The general story was of a rigid rule-follower who harassed her commanders by spouting regulations and challenging them openly when she felt they weren't following the book to the letter.

She pretty much just annoyed anyone who came into contact with her until they were willing to give up a kidney to get her off their ship. It even seemed that some of her promotions had come mostly so they could justify sending her to another post.

"Very well, Lieutenant," I replied to Ingbar. I was starting to like him. He almost made me look good by comparison, and he was refreshingly uncomplicated and boring. Definitely not the guy you wanted to be in your foxhole, but more like the lazy uncle who still lived in your grandparents' basement and would help you score weed as long as you left him alone. Simple. I needed more of that right now.

My head hurt, even a full twelve hours after I'd woken up. I'd drunk a *lot* last night, even for me. Not even my magic hangover pills could keep up. Hoag had to splash water on my face this morning to even get me out of bed.

It could have been humiliating, but I was too shamed already by what I'd seen to care about the added indignity of an uppity, judgmental warrant officer who knew his captain was a raging alcoholic.

At least the whiskey had helped me somewhat forget those videos, even for just a few minutes at a time.

My internal shame parade was broken by an uncharacteristic exclamation from Ingbar. "Sir! Ship detected, bearing oh one oh mark fourteen at point oh three c. Range, four point seven three light seconds."

I perked up. A ship? Seriously? Diverting to waypoint eight had seemed like a great way to break the rigidity and monotony of our mission, but I hadn't expected to actually *find* anything.

"Class?" I asked.

"Unclear. It's running a sensor jammer."

Now I was really alert. Only those with something to hide even had sensor jammers installed on their ships. Probably a smuggler.

"Helm, set a course to intercept," I ordered Yesayan, who looked excited now. Even Lin managed a smile that looked almost predatory.

I hoped they wouldn't get too worked up. If this contact proved to be anything other than a pleasure yacht with a slingshot, it probably outgunned *Persephone*. This patrol could end real quick if we encountered a genuine pirate out here.

CHAPTER 11

Retreat!

"Captain, we have visual."

"Show it," I commanded, and Ingbar dutifully threw the imagery of the ship we'd been chasing on the bridge's main forward viewscreen.

My jaw dropped open. It had been doing a lot of that lately. Next to me, Lin gasped. Even Yesayan grunted in surprise. Ingbar must have returned to his implant's game; I heard no reaction from him.

I'd assumed the ship we'd been closing with for the last three hours had been either a pirate or a smuggler. But it was neither. We were looking at a full-fledged warship, bristling with weaponry, burning its way toward the inner system.

An armed pirate or smuggler would have been a challenge for the lightly armed and armored *Persephone*. But the ship we were seeing now looked to be at least of light cruiser size. And it wasn't Promethean. It was hard to tell at the distance we were at—even the most advanced cameras could only zoom in so far without losing resolution—but it reminded me of Koratan designs.

Koratas was the nation that bordered Prometheus to the galactic north, or Coreward, on the opposite side of Promethean space from Gerson. Koratas and Prometheus had been in a state of cold war for the better part of three centuries now, but it had never risen beyond that except for a few skirmishes with only warning shots fired. The last of those had been twenty-eight years ago.

So, what was a Koratan warship doing this far away from its borders in a worthless system like Gerson? It just made no sense.

What was clear, however, was that *Persephone* would never survive a battle with the enemy ship. This wasn't some storybook where the heroes always won by figuring out some insane scheme to clutch victory from the jaws of defeat. This was real life. And in real life, the bigger ship pretty much always won.

Trying to interdict the Koratan ship would be pure suicide.

"Helm, full stop on the main drive. Execute turnover and burn at full military power back along our current vector!" I commanded.

"But sir," Lin started to argue as I felt the g forces

ramp up and press me in my seat. Full military power was obviously a bit more than the inertial compensators could fully suppress.

"Keep it to yourself, Commander," I snapped, too late realizing that I was taking out my frustrations at what I'd seen earlier in those videos on their very subject. I'd entered the bridge this morning already stressed out of my mind; the enemy warship this evening was just the latest thing to send me spiraling. I tried to recover by at least explaining my order. "That ship could destroy us with barely an effort. The vital thing right now is that we get away to report the sighting and keep our ship and crew alive."

She didn't argue, so I continued in a softer tone. "Send a packet with the sensor logs and a brief summary of the contact to Gerson Station…please."

"Yes, sir," she replied, subdued. It made me feel like a bigger loser than normal.

Pushing aside my self-loathing, I turned to Ingbar. "Lieutenant, is the enemy contact changing vectors to follow us?"

"No, sir. Not to follow, but she is changing to a perpendicular vector and burning back to the outer system."

"Ok," I nodded in relief. "We obviously spooked her, and she's giving up on whatever it is she's doing here. That's good. But let's keep running for a while before we slow our burn. And keep a full sensor sweep going. She might have friends."

If I'd known how prophetic that statement would be, I might have just let that first ship kill us. It would have been so much easier that way.

CHAPTER 12

30% Chance of Death

I swore loudly as Lin finished giving her report. The enemy ship may have been burning on a vector away from us, with the gap widening rapidly, but it had apparently launched a probe behind it that was still close enough to jam our comms. Every attempt to send a message with the contact report to Gerson Station had failed thus far, and Lin had been at it for a full hour.

That meant one of two things. Either the captain of that fleeing ship was worried we might have reinforcements nearby and didn't want us calling them in before he or she could get away, or...

...or they wanted to keep us quiet so that they could kill us before we could report their presence. Which meant there had to be another ship out there. But that same probe was doing a pretty good job of jamming our active sensors as well. So, any other ship might be closer than we thought.

We found it twenty minutes later.

"Contact bearing one seven four mark three relative!" shouted Ingbar in a very unprofessional tone. He must have lost his little implant game; either that or he was actually paying attention to our predicament now. Without being asked, he threw the long-range camera image of the new contact onto the viewscreen.

I swore again. This also looked to be a Koratan warship, but it wasn't a light cruiser. Even my alcohol-ravaged brain recognized it as a Scimitar-class destroyer. It had an acceleration at least twenty percent higher than *Persephone*, and though smaller than the cruiser we'd first seen, it had enough armament to destroy us about fifteen times over before it even had to recharge its weapons.

It would be on us in four hours at current speeds and vectors. It would be in weapons range roughly forty minutes before that. My implant told me all of this; I still wasn't doing math in my head.

"Cheng," I opened a channel to engineering.

"Yes, Captain?" O'Malley responded, stress evident in his voice.

"Can you give me anything more out of those engines?"

His long pause wasn't confidence-inspiring, but I waited the man out. I needed him to have time to think through options. Odd how I was falling back into old habits of command. I'd have to watch out for that. I couldn't delude myself into thinking I was anything more than what I knew myself to be.

"It's risky, Captain," he finally said. "But remember when I was telling you I had some thoughts on increasing the efficiency of the artificial grav and inertial compensators?"

I vaguely recalled ignoring something to that effect at dinner a couple of nights ago. "Sure, Cheng," I lied.

"Well, I haven't tested it yet, but the ion drive itself is capable of another twenty-four percent thrust. We don't go above the set military power only because the compensators can't handle it. But if my plan works, I can probably eke enough efficiency out of the compensators for us to ramp up another sixteen percent or so."

My heart sank. "Cheng, I don't like hearing 'probably' in that sentence."

Another long pause. I knew what he was thinking because I was thinking it too. If he tried what he was proposing, and we ramped up acceleration, and then the compensators failed or even went back to normal levels, we'd all be reduced to jelly stuck to *Persephone's* bulkheads. We wouldn't even have time to process our impending deaths.

"Captain, it's risky, like I said. But I'm seventy percent confident it will work."

Well, seventy percent wasn't great, but I was a

hundred percent confident that Scimitar would blow us to bits as soon as she got in range.

"Ingbar, how much time would that buy us? Enough to reach help?"

The tactical officer shook his head. "It would buy us another twelve hours. But only if we stayed on our current vector, which is aimed only slightly toward the inner system. We'd never get close enough to Gerson Station or any of the other set patrol patterns for the Navy to aid us."

Left unsaid was that the only other two ships out on patrol right now were system patrol boats barely larger than *Persephone*, and even if we had all three of us, the Koratan destroyer would have little trouble turning us all into dust. Gerson Station itself would be hard-pressed to turn back the destroyer and would be absolutely outmatched if that light cruiser joined in. And that assumed those were the only two enemy warships in the system.

But still, it would buy us some time, and the first rule of space warfare was that time meant hope. Besides, I'd wanted to die for a while anyway. I focused on that flippant thought, trying very hard not to think about the other twenty-three people I would be taking down with me.

"Do it," I told O'Malley, and we were committed... with a 30% chance of instantaneous death.

CHAPTER 13

Past Sins

Well, we weren't dead. But we were in a lot of pain. O'Malley's adjustments to the inertial compensators were enough to keep us alive, but we'd been experiencing the equivalent of seven g's for the better part of six hours now. That, coupled with the fact that we'd all been awake for close to twenty hours, made it very hard to think of ways to stay alive.

So far, my command team and I had come up with and rejected a dozen different ideas, all of them focused on escape, not engagement. None were viable.

Finally, after those six hours, I called a break, ordering a temporary decrease in acceleration below what the compensators could handle. This would give us a small amount of time to recover our over-stressed bodies and get something to eat. Ingbar stayed on the bridge, and we called Ensign Stevens up to assist him while I took Lin and Yesayan to the wardroom so we could get a change of scenery.

Hoag brought us our meal there. Unfortunately, for high-g maneuvers, regulations called for a special slurry of high-vitamin liquid rations. Not even my intrepid steward could make *those* taste good.

While we ate—or rather drank—we kept talking through the problem, ignoring the fact that we needed a mental break as much as a physical one.

"What if we reconfigured a probe to mimic our ship's signature and launched it on our current vector, then revectored our thrust and went perpendicular?" Yesayan suggested. It was a variation of two previous suggestions we'd considered and rejected.

"That's a Scimitar class," I replied for the third time. "Latest intel on its sensors suggest it would see right through the ruse, and it could then easily catch us after the vector change."

"Oh, right." It was hard to blame her. We weren't exactly a crack crew of tactical geniuses to begin with, and so many hours at high g's with an accompanying lack of sleep—it was the middle of the night now—were enough to muddle anyone's brain. Luckily the liquid rations had drugs and supplements that should counteract that for a while. The crash, later on, would be spectacular and painful, but they'd been designed with just this type of occasion in mind. I could already feel my brain clearing slightly, though my bar for that was pretty low these days.

"Korgal Manuever?" suggested Lin.

"No," I said. "We don't have any phase torpedoes."

"Right."

"Jacard's Gambit?" Yesayan again.

"No Karatan uniforms on board," Lin said with a frown.

"What about a Chitoran Slide?" I suggested with a hopeful tone, though I knew the answer. It was important to keep the flow of ideas going, even if a real option seemed out of reach.

Lin shook her head. "*Persephone* doesn't have cold reaction thrusters." I knew that, of course, but I'd hoped that maybe someone had installed them without updating my briefing packet or that maybe it was in the part of the packet I still hadn't read. No such luck, apparently.

"Sir, do you mind if I go back to my station? Sometimes I think best when I can view the vectors in a familiar setting?" Yesayan asked.

I nodded to her. "Of course, Lieutenant. Commander Lin and I will join you shortly."

Lin threw me a look but didn't argue, and we waited in silence while Yesayan exited and closed the hatch behind her.

I knew what I wanted to talk to Lin about, though

why I felt the need to do so in the middle of a combat situation I couldn't explain even to myself. But I just couldn't figure out how to start.

Finally, she got sick of waiting and spoke first. "Sir, can I ask you a question? And will you give me an honest answer?"

Uh oh. "Depends," I hedged.

"Why are you here?"

It wasn't the question I'd been expecting, though it was related.

"What do you mean?" I asked, playing for time, much as we were doing with the Koratan destroyer.

"I think you know, sir. You were exonerated of all wrongdoing by the court. And you were on a fast track to flag rank, by all the stories I've heard. But obviously..."

She left the rest unsaid, but it was clear. Obviously, I was now a drunken has-been with no hope for further advancement and no shred of remaining dignity or self-respect. She was right on that, even if she didn't say it out loud. She was wrong about the exoneration.

"Commander," I started. "There's too much to explain. And now really isn't the time."

I saw her frown and hoped she'd drop it. She didn't. "Sir, with all due respect, now may be the only time. And I need to understand. You didn't do anything wrong. The military court said so. So why are you here?"

I grunted in frustration. When I spoke, my voice was sharp and angry, almost a shout, which surprised even me. "Blast the court! They got it wrong, Commander. All wrong. They swept it under the rug because my father-in-law called in some favors, not so that I could walk free but so that he wouldn't be tarnished by association with me. Is that what you want to hear? It was a coverup, all of it. I'm a murderer, plain and simple. Happy?"

"No. You're not." She spoke the words with such conviction that they surprised me and stopped my tirade in its tracks. "I had a friend on *Lancer*. If you hadn't fired when you did, the station could have been destroyed."

"It was a *refugee* ship, Commander. Over five hundred innocents dead. It doesn't matter why I fired, only that I did, and there are families who are gone because of it."

How many times had I tried to articulate that same fact to Carla before she'd left me? It had been my greatest argument that she *should* leave me, even if I wasn't prepared for the way she'd finally done it with that fop Clarington.

"Sir," Lin just wasn't going to let this go. "They wouldn't respond to your hails, wouldn't even use their lights to signal you with flash code. You had no way of knowing it was a refugee vessel, and their captain had put them on a suicide vector with

Bellerophon Station. How were you supposed to…"

"A captain is supposed to know!" I cut her off in exasperation. "There were signs I missed that should have told me what I was dealing with. A ship matching her description fled Langosta space a few weeks before, loaded with Rotingan refugees. If I'd been current on my briefings, I would have known that. They had a sputter in their right engine that no self-respecting pirate or smuggler would have allowed for. And they certainly weren't a warship!"

I stopped, breathing hard, both from the topic and the long hours in heavy gravity. I'd meant to use this time to interrogate Lin about her treatment at the hands of Jessup and Jacobs, but she had somehow turned this around on me to discuss the one topic I most didn't want to discuss with *anyone*.

"But sir…"

"That's enough, Commander!" I snapped. Then I said something monumentally stupid, even for me. "While we're bringing up bad memories, want to tell me what is going on between you and Jacobs? Or Commander Jessup?"

I saw her freeze in her seat next to mine. The color drained from my face, and I wanted to kick myself. I'd meant to bring the subject up lightly, but I'd lashed out, doing anything it took to avoid discussing my crimes. Classic Brad Mendoza move, and another sure piece of evidence that I was one of the worst human beings alive.

After several silent moments, I spoke again, doing my best to soften my voice. Now that the topic had finally come up, I needed to know. "Why didn't you report them, Jessica? Why let them do those things to you?"

"You wouldn't understand," she mumbled, almost under her breath. No denial, just resignation in her tone.

"Try me."

Another long pause. I resisted the urge to keep talking and waited her out. Maybe I still had half a brain left.

"They were going to destroy me," she almost whispered. I waited again, silently willing her to say more.

"Jessup knew about my past—about why I was sent to *Persephone*—and he threatened to tell…" she stopped with a choking sound. Tears streamed down her face. "And Jacobs…well, he's…" She trailed off, shutting her eyes hard.

"Tell what?" I prompted, seizing on the first thing she'd said.

She shook her head. "Sir, you never should have listened to me about that patrol pattern change. I'm broken, and I'll only get you and everyone else on the ship killed. That's just what I do. And I deserve whatever I get."

I opened my mouth to either argue or ask what she

meant, probably both. But then the ship shuddered around us, and the vibration of the deck halted. We had stopped all acceleration and were flying ballistic through space.

CHAPTER 14

A Really Stupid Plan

Remember earlier when I talked about how unreliable the experimental ion drives on the Posiedon-class frigates always were?

Well, up until now, I had dared to hope that *Persephone*'s drives were the exception to that rule. Turns out I was wrong to hope for anything when it came to that blasted ship. Just at the moment we needed her most, she betrayed us.

"We burned out the impeller, Captain!" O'Malley was shouting, even though I was standing right next to him. Apparently, the sound of an ion drive impeller burning out is fairly loud, enough to have seriously damaged the man's hearing.

"How long to fix?" I shouted back, though I knew the answer wouldn't be good.

He shook his head. "We have a spare, but it's not rated for full military power, just enough for us to limp into a shipyard. They made it that way so that it would take up less space in our emergency stores and because the parts are expensive. And *Persephone* is a strictly in-system patrol craft, so they figured we'd never be that far from a station if we got stuck."

In my head, I cursed the Navy and its obsession with saving space and money. I cursed the designers of the Poseidons and, most-of-all, I cursed whatever possessed me to go along with Lin's recommendation to change our patrol pattern. She'd been right about it, but she'd also been right about the fact that it had killed us all. Or rather, *I* had killed us all by agreeing to it. My ship; my fault. I wasn't so far gone I'd forgotten the responsibility of command entirely.

"How long?" I pressed my chief engineer.

"At least four hours for the swap. Have to take apart the starboard conversion bank just to get at the thing."

It was terrible news. In *less* than that time, the enemy would be on us, and *Persephone* and all of us on board her would be so many unconstituted atoms floating in space. It wasn't an exaggeration to say that it would only take that Scimitar-class destroyer a single clear shot, maybe two, to completely destroy us.

"Well, guess I better get to the bridge and see if we can run up the white flag," I said reluctantly. Because we all knew that there was no way that enemy warship was going to let us live. They hadn't responded to any of Lin's communication attempts. They continued to jam us, so it wasn't even clear if they could hear us. It was possible they might relent and accept our surrender now that our acceleration had ceased and if I used the running lights to signal our surrender in flash code. But I doubted it. We were inconvenient witnesses to whatever it was that two Koratan warships were doing in an out-of-the-way system on the edges of Promethean space, far from their own border.

Ironically, now that it was pretty much certain we were dead, I finally had some time to think about just what that might be. Why were these enemy warships so deep in our territory? And why Gerson? It was a worthless system, even in comparison to the other Fringe systems this far from Sol. Most of the people in Prometheus would never see Sol or Earth; it was a six-month journey, even in a top-of-the-line jump ship, just to get there. The general rule was the further you got from Sol, the less value a system had. And Gerson was about as far away as you could get.

The other question that came to mind was just who was *helping* the Koratans. They obviously had our patrol patterns, and our orders were written so rigidly that it was clear to me that someone intended to prevent us from doing exactly what we'd done in varying our pattern so that these Koratans would have a free path into the system.

That suggested Wainwright was in on it. She'd been

prickly when I'd met her, but she hadn't struck me as a traitor. But then again, that was the assessment of a mass murderer, so I wasn't a reliable judge of character.

I said my goodbyes to O'Malley, who couldn't hear me over the ringing in his ears and was already shouting—way too loud—orders to his engineers to start swapping the impeller. It would be too little too late, but at least it gave them something to do while they waited for death. It was good to have hobbies.

It was only a four-minute brisk walk from engineering to the bridge, and in that short time, I came up with nothing even marginally satisfactory to answer my two questions. When I arrived back at my command chair, Lin glanced up at me. By the look in her eyes, I could tell she already knew about the impeller and our hopeless situation...and that she was blaming herself.

"I tried hailing them again, sir," she almost whispered. "No response. And they're still jamming our distress calls. Should we strike the colors?"

"See to it," I said. That was the order to start flashing our running lights in code, signaling our surrender. As I'd already concluded, it wouldn't work. But it was standard operating procedure, and we lost nothing by trying it. Besides, not doing things by the book would probably give Yesayan a coronary and kill her even sooner.

"Any change on that destroyer's vector?" I asked

Ingbar. Another long shot. Maybe they'd gotten bored and turned away.

"No, sir. Two hours and twenty-seven minutes to weapons range intercept."

Great. We had just under two-and-a-half hours left to live. Surprisingly, in that moment, I found myself missing Carla again. When you marry someone, you sort of expect that you're in it with them until the end and that when that end comes, you'll go out together, preferably holding each other to the last second. And even though I'd driven her into the arms of another man, destroyed our marriage, and she'd been clear that she never wanted to hear from me again, it just seemed wrong to be facing my looming death without her by my side. At the same time, I was vastly relieved that she *wasn't* here to die with me and that she would live on. Weird. I figured a team of Navy psychologists could write a fairly thick book about my messed-up brain.

"Any creative ideas, folks?" I asked my bridge crew, shaking off thoughts of my ex-wife.

All four of them—Ensign Stevens had slunk quietly back onto the bridge behind me and was sitting at the usually unoccupied survey console—stayed silent, staring down at their consoles or their hands and refusing to even meet my gaze.

"What if we launched Jacobs at them?" I asked, trying to lighten the mood. Lin flashed a look that I couldn't interpret, but it otherwise fell flat.

Well, this was it then. For six months, I'd more-or-less wanted to die, and the universe had finally heard and was going to give me my wish. Too bad that I would be taking twenty-three other spacers with me. Well, too bad about twenty-two of them; I was actually quite glad Jacobs would die with me after what he'd been doing to Lin. Maybe I could convince her to shoot him a few seconds before we all died, just to get some closure before the end. Probably not; she didn't seem like the type who would want to close out her life with an act of revenge. Maybe *I* could shoot him, just for fun. Where I was going, a five-hundred-and-fifth murder to my name wouldn't matter all that much.

"Uh, sir?" Lin broke the silence timidly. Then she fell quiet. She'd changed since our confrontation in the wardroom; gone entirely were the glimpses of the confident woman I'd seen on other occasions, as if being confronted about her victimhood had brought that aspect of her personality front and center.

I sighed; what a time for her to get shy on me. "Yes, Commander?" I prodded.

"Well, I...uh. Never mind."

I resisted the urge to shake my head and an even greater urge to kick myself. I'd broken her when I needed her the most. Whatever idea she had in her head was probably just as dumb and unworkable as every other one we'd come up with so far, but that didn't mean we shouldn't hear it. And I was *not* going to let Jessica Lin face her death broken like this. She needed to share her idea for her own sake if nothing else.

"Spit it out, XO," I barked, imbuing my voice with all of the command authority it had once carried so naturally. Surprisingly, it worked. Lin looked up at me in something approximating shock, and I watched as her own brain went into command mode as an almost Pavlovian reaction to my order and its tone.

"Yes sir," she answered crisply. "What if we sent full power to the ion drives?"

I furrowed my brow. "What do you mean? The ion drive is broken." What I wouldn't give for a jump drive right then, but the designers of *Persephone* had neglected to install one on such a small warship. It had to be carried attached to a larger ship between systems.

She frowned, and I could see the uncertainty creep back into her face. But she forged ahead. "No, sir...I mean, yes, sir. But if we sent full power to the drive and bypassed all the safeties without an impeller, it would create a feedback loop and a fairly large explosion."

"Okay," I said, trying not to let my doubt through in my voice. "Explain, Commander."

"It could be big enough to destroy that enemy ship."

I shook my head. This really was a dumb idea. Too

bad. "And big enough to kill us. Besides, there's no way that destroyer gets close enough to us to even have their paint scratched, no matter how big of an explosion we make."

"What if there was a way to get them to come closer?" I could see her face harden at my challenge. Good girl. At least my talent for pissing other people off was doing something positive before I finally died.

"OK, I'll bite. How would we do that?" I was now genuinely curious, even though I was still pretty certain it was a stupid plan. But we'd already discarded all the good and even semi-good plans. So stupid was really all we had left.

"What if they thought there was something on board worth getting their hands on, sir?"

I thought about that, examining it from different angles. For a second, my brain fell into old patterns from back when I'd actually been a good captain. Before all the murder and drunkenness. But it only lasted a few seconds and didn't yield anything. I sighed. "Any ideas on how to do that?" I asked her.

"Uh, no, sir," she said sheepishly.

"Well," I said. Maybe I could at least build her confidence up, even if the plan itself was trash. "It was a good attempt. But..."

"King's Cross!" she cried out abruptly, interrupting what would have surely been an uninspiring attempt on my part to console her on her failure. My XO now had a look of wide-eyed excitement and stared around at all of us as if what she'd said should have had obvious implications.

It probably did, but I wasn't picking up on it. King's Cross was the name of a small group of elite intelligence operatives that His Majesty used throughout his kingdom to take on the really sticky messes. But I doubted one had ever seen the need to even get close to Gerson. "Explain, Commander," I ordered again.

"What if the enemy thought we were carrying vital intel that they wanted?"

I wasn't sure where she was going, so I stayed silent, watching the wheels turn in her head.

She started speaking faster. "What if they thought we had a King's Cross operative on board? They would want to capture that operative, not kill them. There are only a handful of King's Cross agents, and each one of them has access to and knowledge of the highest level of Promethean military plans and secrets."

"True," I said, still not getting it. "But how do we convince them we have a King's Cross agent on board when they won't even talk to us? Besides, there's no way a King's Cross agent would ever let themselves be captured. They'd kill themselves first."

"Exactly!" shouted Lin, slamming her hand down

on the comm console in front of her so hard I was surprised she didn't break it—it looked like it had been repaired and patched together so many times, like the rest of *Persephone*, that I was amazed it could even stand up to normal use much less her blatant assault on it.

"The King's Cross," she continued, "wouldn't let themselves get captured. They would self-destruct the ship. Which is exactly what we're going to do."

Now my head was spinning. This felt like a whole lot of circular logic; we were right back to the problem of getting the enemy close enough before they destroyed us for our self-destruction to do any good by maybe damaging them.

Luckily, Lin chose to ignore my confused look and kept talking. "If we can somehow show the enemy that we plan to blow ourselves up, it might make them think that we have something to keep away from them."

"I don't know," Ingbar said for the first time, somehow managing to sound just as bored as he always did. "It would be a huge leap of logic for them to see our self-destruction as a sign we have a King's Cross agent on board."

"Not if we broadcast the Death Cry," Lin said with a grin.

Silence. I'd call it stunned silence, but for me, it was more of a confused silence. Until it wasn't, when the little light inside my brain finally sputtered to life.

"It just might work," I muttered. The King's Cross Death Cry was a thing of legend. I wasn't even sure it was real. But supposedly, when a King's Cross operative was about to die, they broadcast a very specific message that served two purposes. First, it told their enemy whom they had bested, like a sign of respect. Second, it told their enemy they only had a short time left to live. Because, again, based on rumor, the Death Cry was also a signal to all other King's Cross agents to hunt down and destroy whoever had killed their brother or sister.

Even if we had a King's Cross agent on the ship, the Death Cry wouldn't really work when all our comms were being jammed. But if the enemy was leaving just enough of the jamming open to listen to our attempts to communicate, even if they refused to respond, it might work. Assuming, of course, that the Koratans had also heard the rumors about the Death Cry. There were a lot of 'ifs' in this plan.

"So," I said slowly, "we broadcast the Death Cry and then make it look like we're going to blow up the ship, which should be somewhat easy because we really *do* plan to do that. And we hope they fall for it and disable and board us instead of just destroying us and being done with it?"

"Yes, sir!" Lin almost shouted again in her enthusiasm. It was the polar opposite of the woman who had reacted like a beaten dog in the corridor with Jacobs and who had been sulking in silence the last few hours on the bridge. And suddenly, I had insight into what had made Lin such a great officer before whatever it was that had ended her career progression...and a glimpse of what she could be *again* if given the chance. And I could tell that she was thinking along similar lines. It felt strangely good to see her confidence flourish like that.

"And then when they get close enough to board us, we *do* destroy the ship and take them with us?" I asked.

Despite her enthusiasm, it wasn't a stupid plan; it was a *really* stupid plan. But it was also the only plan I'd heard today that might actually work. Besides, a stupid plan for a stupid ship and its stupid captain was probably fitting.

"But how will we destroy the ship if they've already disabled us?" Ingbar objected. His voice made it clear he really didn't like the plan. But it was a legitimate question. "And how do we get off the ship before it blows up without them seeing the escape pods?" Another very legitimate question, unless Lin was as suicidal as I sometimes got.

I looked over at my XO to see how she would answer. She was grinning widely. "Come on, Captain, Lieutenant; you expect me to come up with *all* the ideas?"

Seeing what Jessica Lin could be made me hate Jessup and Jacobs even more for what they had robbed her of, and disappointed for whatever had happened on *Ordney* that had derailed her career. Just as important, seeing her enthusiasm lit something inside of me that I'd tried very hard to forget about over the last six months.

"Someone get O'Malley up here," I said. "You may need to shout."

CHAPTER 15

Not the Way I Planned It

You know how when a beautiful girl is happy, she gets even more beautiful? Well, Lin was absolutely breathtaking right now. I hadn't seen her happy since I'd boarded Persephone just days before, and now she was practically giddy. It suited her.

With some prompting from me, O'Malley had filled in one other part of the plan for us. If we shunted all reactor power to the backup batteries, he'd surmised, we should be able to store enough charge to overload the ion drives at the right time, even if the reactor itself was disabled.

So, the first problem—how we would blow up our ship and the Koratan destroyer—was mostly solved. And the solution to the second problem, that of how we'd get off the ship undetected *before* blowing it up, surprisingly came from Ingbar.

One thing we'd all more-or-less forgotten was that

Persephone, for all her faults and weaknesses, was, in fact, a warship. She would have no chance in a standup fight with any other warship, mind you, but she *did* have missiles in her magazines. Ingbar's idea was simple: launch a broadside toward the enemy destroyer. The enemy would easily swat the missiles out of space, but it might provide just enough distraction and sensor scatter to hide the launch of our escape pods.

The only problem was that someone would have to stay behind. The ship couldn't destroy itself, and if we didn't destroy it, we wouldn't be able to damage or destroy the Koratan vessel, and it would easily then find and hunt down our escape pods.

That might have been the easiest problem to solve so far. I would stay. As the only mass murderer on the ship *and* as her captain, it only made sense. However, I surprised myself. For all of my self-loathing and even genuine desire over the last six months to end it all, I found that wasn't the reason that I readily volunteered to be the one to stay behind. In fact, I found myself oddly melancholy at the idea of my impending death.

No, the real and surprising reason I so readily agreed to go down with my ship wasn't so that I could die. Rather, as I looked at Lin, O'Malley, Yesayan, Stevens, and even Ingbar, I realized almost with chagrin that what I really wanted was for *them* to live. It was a strange epiphany for someone who had killed over five hundred innocents, to be willing to give up my own life for the sake of five people I'd only known for a few days.

In fact, my only real regret was that I couldn't keep Jacobs on the ship with me. He'd probably find a way to mess up the whole plan if I tried.

Which wasn't to say I wasn't going to do something about the man. As Lin and the other officers worked out the finer points of the plan—even Stevens had a few mildly helpful suggestions—I used my implant to compose a note to my ex-father-in-law. Oliphant might be an ogre with no redeeming qualities, but he *was* an admiral with a duly sworn duty to His Majesty's Navy. My note outlined the situation with Jacobs and Lin, as well as the involvement of Jessup—I learned from the notes in my orders that said scumbag was still alive and commanding a destroyer in the Linford system. To my note, I attached the video evidence from Jessup's logs. I still didn't know why the man had recorded the encounters, and I really didn't *want* to know. I could only hope it was enough proof to put Jessup and Jacobs away for a very long time and keep any blowback away from Lin herself.

I loaded the note onto the memory of two of the escape pods with auto-routing instructions so it would reach someone at naval headquarters and hopefully be forwarded to Carla's jerk of a dad.

Now, all that was left to do was to wait. We had twenty minutes before the enemy reached weapons range, and we had to time things just right. If we made signs of self-destruction and broadcast the Death Cry too early, it would give the Koratan captain time to think things through and realize how unlikely it was that a King's Cross agent would be traveling on a piece of junk like the *Phony*. If we broadcast it too late, the destroyer would have already launched a set of ship killers at us, and we'd be dead.

Eighteen minutes passed, simultaneously the longest and shortest eighteen minutes of my life. Then the last two minutes became very frantic indeed.

"Send the message," I commanded, and Lin pressed a single button on her console. We'd already drafted the fake Death Cry message, full of all sorts of fun little threats against the enemy on behalf of the King's Cross—Ensign Stevens surprisingly had quite a foul vocabulary—and loaded it in the buffer so it was ready to send.

Then, O'Malley sent a surge from the reactor to the ion drive. It was a big enough surge that it would show up on the enemy destroyer's sensors. But it was just under the threshold—we fervently prayed —to actually overload the broken drive and kill us all. The enemy would hopefully see it and interpret it as a failed attempt to self-destruct.

The power surge didn't kill us, and we all breathed a collective sigh of relief. Now though, we had to see if it worked. We held our breath again as the Scimitar entered weapons range.

"They launched a scrambler!" Ingbar cried out in the most animated voice I'd ever heard him use. That was good; a scrambler was a disabling weapon meant to target and disrupt our reactor's containment field, shutting it down. The physics of how they work is complex, but they work quite well, especially against lightly armored ships. It meant the enemy had taken our bait. We'd have about three minutes until it hit us.

"Fire full broadside," I ordered, my voice a bit calmer than my tactical officer's. It helped that a full broadside for *Persephone* was only three missiles, and they were small, short-range anti-ship missiles that wouldn't do much damage to anything larger than a lifeboat.

The second-to-last part of the plan had arrived. We'd already loaded everyone but the officers into the pods. O'Malley was down in engineering making the final arrangements for the real self-destruct sequence, which I would have to go to engineering to execute. He would shortly board an escape pod near his station with the rest of his engineers.

Now it was time for my bridge crew to board theirs. Only Lin and Ingbar were left. I'd already ordered Stevens and Yesayan to a pod over their protest.

This was the awkward part. Or I assumed it would be, and I was half right. Ingbar threw me a sharp salute but said nothing as he left the bridge to board the pod that already held the other two officers. That left me and Lin alone.

Lin had tears in her beautiful eyes. Mass-murderer-about-to-die-and-go-straight-to-hell I may have been, but if I had to go out, I guess going out with those eyes crying for me was about the best I could hope for.

She said nothing but stood ramrod straight and saluted. Then she broke down into a vocal sob and threw herself at me, surprising me with a hug.

It was over quickly, and she rushed off the bridge and into the pod with the others before I could say anything. It was a bit disappointing to be robbed of any heroic last words, but I probably would have screwed them up anyway.

Now, I turned to leave the bridge myself and made my way to engineering, but not before checking to see that all of the escape pods had launched. Only one remained, and it showed empty; even had I wanted to, I would never have the time to reach it after I executed the self-destruct. The ship would be gone in seconds.

The lights cut out as the scrambler hit *Persephone* and took out the main reactor. I navigated the darkened corridors, lit now only by emergency lamps, so it took me a couple of extra minutes to get to engineering. At least the dim lights had their own energy storage and wouldn't steal power from the backup battery. We'd need all of that to keep our sensors going and then blow the ion drive.

O'Malley had rigged a repeater display down in the engine room so I could see the sensor picture. That way, I could time *Persephone's* destruction at the exact moment the enemy ship closed to boarding range. With luck, it would destroy them along with us. At the very least, it should damage them enough that hunting down our escape pods would be the least of their concerns. And that light cruiser was far enough away now that it was unlikely to reach us before a rescue from Gerson. If our comms couldn't reach the station, the light of an ion drive going critical surely would.

Engineering had no chairs—stupid designers—so I sat on the deck with my back to a low console to await the arrival of the Koratan destroyer and my well-deserved death.

I heard the footstep behind me only an instant before I felt the crushing blow to my skull, and everything went dark.

CHAPTER 16

An Unlikely Hero

I woke up to a flashing red light through my closed eyelids and the really annoying sound of something beeping. My first thought was that it was way too early for my alarm to be going off. My second thought was that I must be waking up after a bender. Any moment, I expected to feel the cold splash of water on my face as that sadist Hoag forcefully roused me before breakfast. That thought made me hungry.

It took a minute or two for me to clear my head and open my eyes. I had a massive headache, and my scalp felt funny, as if something was caked on it. Like blood? My mind cleared a little, and I remembered just enough to expect to find myself in engineering when my vision finally cleared. But when I blinked the tears away, I was shocked to see the spartan accouterments of a standard Navy escape pod.

What in the...?

Panic surged through me. If I was in an escape pod, that meant no one had been there to destroy *Persephone*! And without that, the enemy ship would surely kill all of us any second. I scrambled to the viewport but could see nothing through it but the dark of space and a few scattered stars, even after blinking several times to try and further clear my vision.

Then the red flashing light caught my attention. The comm. I pressed it, if for no other reason than to stop that incessant blinking and beeping.

"—tain? Captain? Do you read? Captain Mendoza, do you read?" I was overjoyed to hear Lin's voice—at least someone else out there was still alive—and I felt an oddly warm surge at the obvious concern in her tone before I realized that concern was probably for my failed mission and our impending doom rather than for my well-being.

"I'm here, Lin. What happened?" It was a stupid question. At least I was consistent.

"Captain!" she exclaimed, relief filling her voice and sending a warm feeling through me. It doubled when I remembered the hug she'd given me on the bridge before I was to selflessly sacrifice myself to save her and everyone else.

Then I went cold again. Something with that plan had obviously gone very wrong. However...

"It worked!" Lin was saying. "It was Ingbar. He knocked you out, dragged you to the last pod, and then launched it right before that destroyer got close enough to be damaged by the self-destruct. Then he blew up *Persephone* and took the Koratans with him."

"Ingbar?" I tried to ask, but Lin kept talking over me.

"We thought your pod had been destroyed too. It took us an hour to find its sensor return through all the wreckage. But its status shows as damaged. You lost some of your oxygen."

"Ingbar?" I asked dumbly again. Of all the people on *Persephone* to play the hero, he was the *last* one I would have expected. The guy hadn't seemed to have a motivated bone in his body.

Surprising. Somehow inspiring. I sort of both loved and hated him right now.

"With that destroyer gone, so is the jamming," Lin continued, probably having figured out by now I wasn't going to say anything intelligent in response. "Gerson Station dispatched rescue ships four hours ago, and they should be here before the pods run out of air."

Wait, hadn't she just said my damaged pod had lost some of its oxygen reserves? Maybe I would get to die after all.

But it turned out I wouldn't get my grand exit from mortality. With only one person on board, my pod had just enough air to get me rescued.

I found I wasn't all that disappointed.

CHAPTER 17

The King's Cross

I sat quietly in the outer waiting room of the naval offices on Gerson Station. I'd been released from the med bay after a quick treatment for the nasty head wound Ingbar had given me—for a hero trying to save my life, he sure came close to killing me—and had been immediately summoned to Wainwright's office.

But I arrived to find the normal spacer at the reception desk gone. The entire place looked deserted. I could hear muffled voices in Wainwright's office, but no one answered when I knocked. So, I sat down and waited.

My entire crew, minus Ingbar, had come through our ordeal safely. Even Jacobs, though I had other plans for him.

Technically, none of them were my subordinates anymore; we no longer had a ship to be captain and crew of, but I felt oddly protective of them nonetheless. Even the ones I'd not even met in my short time on *Persephone*. So, I'd checked on each and every one of them in the med bay of the station before I'd let the doctors treat my head. The only one I hadn't been able to find was Lin, and no one knew where she was. Members of the crew thought she'd made it to the station OK, and I had seen her briefly hovering over me in my few lucid moments on the rescue ship, but she had never arrived at the med bay. It was strange and more than a little concerning, and it occupied my thoughts as I sat waiting.

The door to Wainwright's office finally opened, but it wasn't the grumpy captain I saw standing there. It was the red-headed civilian woman from the transport that had brought me to Gerson just days before—the one who had given me the look of death when she'd caught me checking her out. She was pretty, but now that I'd seen Jessica Lin, there really wasn't a comparison.

"Ah, Captain Mendoza," she said with a nod. She stepped out into the antechamber, and I was shocked to see Wainwright exiting behind her, or more accurately, *being* exited. Two burly enlisted men held the captain by each arm and bodily dragged her from her office and through the outer hatch. I was too surprised to say anything, and Wainwright didn't meet my startled gaze.

"Captain, if you will?" the red-haired woman said, gesturing into Wainwright's office.

Stunned into silence, I stood and followed her in. She took up position in Wainwright's chair and indicated I should take the chair across from her. It was surreal, as she was wearing civilian garb and sitting in a naval station commander's chair.

"Who are you?" I finally found my voice. My head was pounding still, but the question didn't sound quite as stupid as was the norm for me.

She smirked, a sort of half smile that reminded me of the proverbial cat who had just eaten a mouse. "You caused quite a stir over the last few days, Captain Mendoza," she said, ignoring my question. "First, you disobeyed direct orders and took your ship to the wrong waypoint. Then you discovered a Koratan incursion into the Gerson system. Then, somehow, you managed to take out a destroyer ten times your size with a broken-down ship. I have it on good authority that was *Persephone's* one and only verified kill in her seventy-three years of service, and it was the first enemy naval warship kill for our entire *Navy* in the last decade! And after all of that, you managed to get yourself knocked out and thrown into an escape pod for a last-minute rescue."

She stopped, letting all that hang in the air. It was a fun little recap of what I already knew. But I decided to keep my mouth shut and wait her out.

The redhead smirked again. "Don't worry, Captain. You're not in trouble, at least not with me. That was some bravery and ingenuity the likes of which

I can appreciate. If you weren't the Butcher of Bellerophon, you'd probably be getting a medal after all this."

She paused again, eyeing me with a raised eyebrow. I guessed it was my turn to speak.

"Who are you?" I repeated my earlier question. So much for not sounding as stupid as usual.

"Tell me, Captain," she asked, ignoring my second attempt to interrogate her, "whose idea was it to use the King's Cross Death Cry to trick the Koratans? Was it Commander Lin?"

"Depends on who's asking," I said cautiously. I wasn't about to throw Lin under the bus if this strange woman had some issue with how we'd stayed alive.

Now she smiled with *both* sides of her mouth. "Relax, Captain. As I said, I'm not here to get you or Lin in trouble. Though some of my colleagues don't like it when someone else pretends to be a member of our little group, you're in luck that I actually got a kick out of your approach. Be sure to tell your XO that I'm impressed and that she should consider this redemption for what happened on *Ordney*."

I seized upon that and opened my mouth to ask her to explain what *had* happened to Lin on *Ordney* that had derailed her career, but then I stopped. Had this strange woman just admitted that *she* was an agent of the King's Cross?

Now, her expression turned serious. "In all honesty, Captain, you and your crew did exceptionally well. I was already here investigating rumors that someone in Gerson was passing on top-secret information to the enemy, and you solved the case for me. I shouldn't be telling you this, but just a few months ago, there was a large deposit of stellarium discovered in Gerson's asteroid belt. We'd managed to keep it quiet, but the Koratans somehow found out and were keen to move in and take the system."

My mouth fell open; that was my go-to move now. Stellarium was the rarest metal known to humanity. Just an ounce was worth enough to buy a modest-size *town* on Prometheus. And it was the absolute best material for the manufacturing of warship hulls; it had properties that made it resistant to energy weapons and even allowed it to absorb a small nuclear detonation without breaking apart. The entire Promethean Navy didn't have a single ship with a Stellarium hull; it was rumored no one did in the Fringe systems. The only known deposits were all much closer to Sol.

If Gerson had a deposit of the metal, and depending how large, it had just gone from the most worthless system in all of humanity to perhaps the most valuable.

I had so many follow-up questions, but my head hurt too much, so I just sat there with my mouth agape.

"I see I have your attention," she said wryly. "We

kept this thing so secret that not even the Navy was supposed to know. We knew that the second we moved a fleet toward Gerson, it would alert everyone in the Fringe to our discovery. The plan was to quietly move a few ships into the system over the next two months and then send Third Fleet by on their normal patrol of the outer territories and have them stay here.

"But we got intel that someone in the system had leaked the discovery, though we didn't know to whom they were leaking it. It appears now it was to the Koratans. And your decision to divert from your patrol pattern and actually *find* the enemy, along with the strangely strict wording of your orders, pointed us toward Wainwright as the turncoat. She just confessed...after some persuasion. Somehow, she'd found out about the stellarium and decided to cash in and reap some of the massive windfall it will create by selling us out to the enemy."

I said nothing. I was getting unexpectedly good at looking like an idiot with my mouth open, so I decided to keep practicing that skill.

"Well, Captain, I can see that I've rendered you speechless." Then her smile abruptly disappeared. "But we have another problem that I need to discuss with you: Lieutenant Commander Lin's future."

My heart sank. I should have known something was wrong when no one had seen Lin since arriving on the station. It was enough to break me from my silence.

"Where is she? What have you done with her?" I used my command voice.

The King's Cross agent wasn't impressed. She smiled sadly. "I've done nothing with her apart from sequestering her in a cabin on the station where no one will find her. It's actually *you* who has done something to her."

"Me? What are you talking about?" I demanded, my voice losing its professional tone.

"That message you loaded into the escape pod memories," she said with a frown. "It was downloaded into the station naval computer and read by multiple personnel here *and* forwarded to the outer communication beacon before I could intercept it."

"So what?" I asked angrily, surprising myself at how worked up I was getting, even in my half-dazed state. "The Navy needs to know what's been happening to her. It's wrong on so many levels. I did what I did to make sure she gets justice, and I would do it again. Even the King's Cross can't suppress that kind of information." They probably could, but I was pretty ticked off right then.

"Calm down, Captain!" she snapped, all smiles gone. "Remember to whom you speak!" Her command voice was better than mine. Then her tone softened. "Besides, I'm trying to *help* you and Lin, not hurt you. But unfortunately, the Navy already knew what was happening on *Persephone*."

My mouth fell open again. Yes, again. I was becoming predictable.

She frowned and nodded. "You really didn't read the personnel records for your new command, did you? Petty Officer Nedrin Jacobs. Except that his mother's maiden name is Worthington."

My heart fell into my stomach. "You mean...?" I couldn't even finish the question.

She nodded sadly again. "Yes, *those* Worthingtons. Nedrin Jacobs is the nephew of our Royal Highness, His Majesty King Charles the Eighth of the Royal House of Worthington, Defender of the Realm, and Lord of the Federated Systems of Prometheus. And my boss."

Oh no. I was screwed.

CHAPTER 18

A Murderer's Death

So, I guess that being a scoundrel and a rapist was enough to get you knocked from an officer's rank down to enlisted, no matter who your mommy was, but not enough to get you court-martialed or even stopped from continuing your crimes…at least if you're the King's nephew.

Now, Jacobs' blatant approach to me on that first day on *Persephone* made perfect sense. Except, idiot that I was, I'd never actually read his file. So, I had no idea the fire I was playing with when I'd exposed him and Jessup for what they'd done to Lin. By the way, it really had been Jessup who had started the whole affair, using some sort of leverage he held over Lin to force her into his bunk, but he'd convinced Jacobs to join in, mostly to keep himself safe by association. Then he'd filmed it all probably to make sure Jacobs couldn't weasel out of charges without also getting Jessup free. And it had worked.

And as Agent of the King's Cross Heather Kilgore had pointed out to me in Wainwright's former office, by accusing the King's nephew of rape, I had quite literally guaranteed my own death and that of Lin. The accusation needed to be quieted quickly, lest it become a scandal for the Crown. In fact, Kilgore told me she expected to receive the orders herself to kill the two of us as soon as the King got wind of my message to Oliphant. That was if Oliphant didn't order it himself first. There was already a fast courier ship on its way to Prometheus with the news, along with an urgent request for reinforcements against the Koratan incursion.

I suppose it should have surprised me that my ex-father-in-law was in on the whole thing; he'd known for months what was happening to Lin, and other women, at the hands of Jessup and Jacobs, and he'd done nothing. It *should* have surprised me, but I'd never liked Carla's dad, even when I'd been crazy about her.

All that was highly unfortunate. But there was one small way in which fortune smiled on us. Heather Kilgore had a conscience. Or perhaps, as she'd said, Lin had just really impressed her with the genius plan to save the crew of *Persephone* and destroy that Scimitar. Either way, Kilgore had decided to help us, so long as we were out of her sight and reach before she got the official orders to kill us, that was.

Apparently, her morality only extended to bending her orders, not breaking them.

And that's how Captain Brad Mendoza and Lieutenant Commander Jessica Lin died, me from complications related to my head wound, and her from radiation poisoning from *Persephone's* destruction that somehow hadn't affected anyone else in her escape pod.

It was strange being dead. After sort of wishing for it for a while, it was surprisingly anticlimactic. I imagine there was a small service of some kind. Maybe Carla even cried into Clarington's shoulder. I hope it soiled his dress uniform.

But I guess that either way, it didn't matter to me. I wasn't in attendance. I was dead.

Funny, though, just a few hours after my meeting with Kilgore, a small merchant freighter left Gerson Station. More accurately, it was stolen by parties unknown. On board were two individuals with identity papers that proved they'd never been part of the Promethean Navy.

One was an absolutely stunning young woman with a still-secret and complicated past, and now a new confidence and zest for life after she'd saved the lives of twenty-two others with her brilliance. And the second was an unshaven drunk. Did I mention he was also a mass murderer? Or maybe he wasn't anymore. I'm not actually sure how new lives work. Do past sins carry over?

Luckily, the Navy didn't have any ships handy at the station to send after the stolen craft, or I might have found out. And then another funny thing happened. No one could actually figure out to whom the stolen ship had belonged in the first place. It was a nice ship; it even had a jump drive, a rarity for a craft so small. But its registry and prior ownership were nowhere to be found. And without a wounded party, no one could really muster up the enthusiasm or even a good excuse to chase it.

Apparently, the King's Cross really can do just about anything they want.

My only regret in the whole affair was that I didn't get to add a five-hundred-and-fifth murder to my tally. Jacobs got to live and apparently keep doing terrible things to people. But at least Lin was free of him, and her spark was back. And maybe I'd find him someday and shoot him anyway, just for fun. Murderers get to do stuff like that. Or better yet, maybe I'd simply hold him while Lin shot him.

Either way, life would never be the same. But my old life ended terribly anyway. Maybe the second time around would be better.

But let's be honest; I'm pretty sure I'll find a way to screw it up.

THE END OF BOOK ONE

Enjoyed this book? Read the rest of the *Dumb Luck and Dead Heroes* series today! Available on Kindle, Paperback, and Audiobook.

Don't ever miss a new release!

Sign up now for Skyler's newsletter and get access to new release updates, free content, and great deals.

Go to www.skylerramirez.com/join-the-club

BOOKS BY SKYLER RAMIREZ

Dumb Luck & Dead Heroes

The Worst Ship in the Fleet

The Worst Spies in the Sector

The Worst Pirate Hunters in the Fringe

The Worst Rescuers in the Republic

The Worst Detectives in the Federation

The Worst Traitors in the Confederacy

The Worst Fugitives in the Star Nation (Coming Soon)

A Star Nation In Peril

Set in the same universe as *Dumb Luck and Dead Heroes*.

Rogue Agent

Suicide Mission

Assassin's Flight (Coming Soon)

The Brad Mendoza Chronicles

Short stories set in the same universe as *Dumb Luck and Dead Heroes*.

Saving the Academy

Battle for Poe

Siege of Jalisco

The Four Worlds

The Four Worlds: The Truth

The Four Worlds: Subversion

The Four Worlds: Wrath of Mars (coming 2024)

Revolution: A Four Worlds Story

ABOUT THE AUTHOR

Skyler S. Ramirez

 I just love writing. It's as simple as that. My goal is to write books that my readers enjoy and that celebrate everyday imperfect heroes. I want to show that everyone, no matter how life has dealt with them or how they've dealt with life, deserves a second chance and can go on to do amazing things. Just look at Brad and Jessica in Dumb Luck and Dead Heroes or Jinny and Tyrus in The Four Worlds.

It's important to me that everyone be able to read my books, including my teenage children, so I purposefully leave out any swearing or graphic scenes. In this, I follow a tradition set by many (far better) writers before me, most notably in my life, Louis L'Amour. I can only aspire to write even half as good as Mr. L'Amour!

As for the personal side, I live in Texas with my

wife and four children (and often a revolving door of exchange students), and I work for a major tech company for my day job. But writing is my passion, and I often toil into the early hours of morning, especially on the weekends, and it's all worth it when I see people enjoy my books.

Thanks for reading.

Printed in Great Britain
by Amazon